LOSING IT

LINDSAY FAITH RECH

was born Lindsay Faith Resnick in 1978 in Philadelphia, Pennsylvania. When she was nine, her family moved to the Bucks County suburbs. After high school, she attended Rider University in Lawrenceville, New Jersey, where she studied writing and theater. During her junior year, she began dating her future husband, Scott Rech, whom she married five months after graduating with top honors with a degree in fine arts. Prior to realizing her longtime dream of becoming a published author, Lindsay had her own column in a New Jersey newspaper and worked as an assistant editor for a chain of news magazines in Bucks County. Today, she writes full-time.

LOSING IT

Lindsay Faith Rech

**RED
DRESS
INK**
™

First edition October 2003

LOSING IT

A Red Dress Ink novel

ISBN 0-373-25037-1

Visit Red Dress Ink at www.reddressink.com

Printed in U.S.A.

To my husband, Scott, for his brave optimism
and complete belief in this book

ACKNOWLEDGMENTS

An entire world of thanks
to my wonderful parents, Hillary and Ivan,
for everything they have done for me and for always
being proud of their children. Many, many thanks also to my
talented and hilarious brother, Matthew, and my extraordinary
grandparents, Doris and Lenny. And much appreciation to the
rest of my family and all of my friends, especially Jill,
who has been making the world more fun since I was ten
and who always said this day would come.

My tremendous gratitude
also goes out to everyone at Red Dress Ink
and Harlequin, particularly my gracious editor
Margaret Marbury, for giving me this unbelievable chance
to live out a dream. Last, but far from least, a very special
thank you to Zareen Jaffery for all her kind help
and encouragement during this exciting new process.

CHAPTER ONE

It was the whitest room she had ever seen. Floors white, walls white, even the shadows were white—everything dripping in milky obscurity except for those two stubborn colors. But the metal post that stretched from the bed to the ceiling was hardly a color, really—just a noticeable variation in the blanched monotony of the room. She heard the woman next to her choking back tears, but why? It was only a lock of hair—beautiful hair, orangey-gold like honeyed fire. It was color on her pillow. Brilliant color. Color that both shocked and softened the glaring, staring, commanding and unforgiving white. Her cry was haunting, relentless and a little sad. But she didn't say a word, and it was impossible to understand what bothered her. Maybe she cried because the whispers were frightening. But they only spoke of senseless things, like shamrocks and motives and cafés. And some girl named Erin and a Davey boy who had probably broken her heart. Or was it Chevy—the whispers seemed to know something about him. Shamrocks, Davey, Erin, Chevy, motives and cafés. And there were numbers, too. Numbers listed like on the inside of a fortune cookie—6, 18, 11, 19, 94. And always in that order. They taunted the silence, these whispers, filling the room with their threatening anonymity. They had no faces, no name tags, no excuses for forcing her and Honey Fire to listen but not ask questions. But maybe it wasn't the whispers. Maybe she cried because her pillow smelled like tonsils and biopsies or because it was cold in the room with no color but the fire she gave it, and the burning provided no warmth. Or perhaps she was crying at the burden of being the only real color in this blank vault of whispers—because bearing that burden meant she must have done something punishable to deserve it. *At 6, 18…window…Davey's Café.* They circled the room like vultures—each number, each word, each unfamiliar name. *Corner…Shamrock…Baltimore.* But they were no longer senseless nothings, these whispers filling her head, because they knew a name that she knew too. And the whispers murmured *Diana*…and she realized that she was completely alone. The other woman, crying at the cold with the honeyed fire hair—the one who'd brought color to the blankness—was her. It was *her* lock of brilliance, *her* orangey gold, *her* haunting tears, *her* biopsy pillow. And *this*—all of it—was her punishment, her own vault of vultures hinting at what she had done. But all the hints in the whispering world could never tell her why.

At 6:18 p.m., on Friday, July 11th, Diana Nicole Christopher crashed her 1994 Chevy Nova through the front window of Davey's Café on the corner of Erin Avenue and Shamrock Street in Baltimore. No motive has been determined.

CHAPTER TWO

Thursday, May 29th
1:09 p.m.

Today is the first day of the rest of your life.

"I always get the shitty ones," Diana complained, squeezing her fortune cookie into a fistful of crumbs and blowing them onto her plate like ashes.

"That's why you can't find a decent job," Mrs. Christopher said, assuming that look of motherly concern that always pissed Diana off.

"Why, Mom? Because Ping's Palace only serves me the stupid clichés?"

"No, because you think sayings like 'Today is the first day of the rest of your life' are worthless."

"And they're not?"

"Diana, grab your purse," Mrs. Christopher said with a disapproving frown as she slid her chair out from the table. "And tuck your shirt in next time we go out to lunch."

"I can't," Diana said, standing up. "My jeans are un-buttoned."

"Diana," her mother began once they were outside, and far enough away from the judgmental ears of anyone who might spurn her for having an overweight daughter, "I've offered you money to buy yourself clothes that fit you. No daughter of mine needs to walk around without decent clothes to wear. Now I've told you. Being heavy does *not* have to make you unattractive. You have a pretty face." Mrs. Christopher reached out to touch Diana's cheek, but the pretty face pulled away, tired of the conversation—it was always the same. "So, until you lose weight," Mrs. Christopher continued, reciting the same old lines from a script that hadn't changed in twenty years, "it's all in how you present yourself—in how you walk, in how you dress." She reached into her wallet. "Here's a fifty. Now, stand up straight."

Diana put the money away, catching her new cubic zirconia ring on the less-than-spacious jean pocket that stretched tightly across her hip.

"Oh, dear, Diana, why?" her mother begged, adopting her signature expression of confusion. Diana recognized the look immediately—that unique blend of horror and hurt that could shame any overweight and irreversibly insecure thirty-something daughter into feeling guilty and hopelessly idiotic without a single clue as to what for.

"Because I thought it was pretty?" Diana often answered her mother in the form of a question so that if her answer were wrong, which it usually was, she wouldn't appear as presumptuous about life as she would if she'd answered with assurance.

"Honey, you should be spending your tip money on clothes you can breathe in, not jewelry that you don't need. Besides, you're gonna have a real hard time finding a man with *that* thing on your finger. It looks like an engagement ring! If you *have* to wear it, at least wear it on your right hand."

Diana suspected that her mother was mocking her— by acting like there was any chance in hell that the men would be lining up for her if she *weren't* wearing this "engagement" ring. Besides, she couldn't wear it on her right hand. She'd ordered it from the home shopping channel, and the only finger it fit on when it came to her door was the one typically reserved for engagement rings and wedding bands. But she wasn't about to tell her mother that one of her ring fingers was fatter than the other. She just wanted to make it home without any further attacks on her dignity.

"Thanks for lunch, Mom. We'll do it again next week, okay?" A week was the general length of recovery time she required after lunch with her mother. It was practically doctor's orders.

"You've got it," Mrs. Christopher agreed, sliding into her shiny new black Volvo and starting it up. "And remember," she said, grasping the door handle, "today is the first day of the rest of your life." Diana rolled her eyes. "I mean it, Diana. Find a job that makes you happy." Diana hated the way her mother said the word "happy," probably because her voice robbed it of meaning. "Maybe you'll have some good news for me by this time next Thursday."

"Bye, Mom," Diana said, forcing a mini smile. "And thanks for the clothes money. I'll pay you back when I can."

"You can pay me back by losing some of that weight so you don't keep breaking my heart *and* my wallet every time we go to lunch." Mrs. Christopher laughed, stopping only after she noticed that Diana wasn't even faking mild amusement. "Oh, I'm only kidding, sweetie. Relax! And listen," she continued, closing her car door as she pressed the automatic window button, "say hi to that nice old lady upstairs for me, will you? What's her name again?"

"Mrs. Bartle. And it's downstairs," Diana corrected her, for what seemed like the millionth time.

"Uh-huh," Mrs. Christopher said, smiling. But Diana knew the correction was about as important to her as the atomic weight of plutonium. "Take care, dear." And as her mother drove away, with the sun glinting off of her newest status symbol, Diana opened the door of her nine-year-old Chevy and, with her freshly revised mental list of loserhood, wondered when she would stop being a disappointment to the only real family she had left.

"I mean, how did she know I *wasn't* engaged? I could have a man in my life without her knowing about it." Diana wished her words were true. The having a man part would be better, of course, but a life free from her mother's meddling wasn't a bad wish either, since neither were very likely to happen.

"Oh, child, you're too young to be worried about all that! You'll meet someone." Mrs. Bartle was always so reassuring. And the best part about her was that she was honest and really believed what she said—that a thirty-two-year-old, overweight waitress at a truck-stop diner, who hated her body more than she hated her work, and who ate stale strawberry shortcake on her coffee break because free desserts were the only real benefits her job entitled her to, was actually *young* and likely to marry.

"Mrs. Bartle, how did you meet your husband?" Diana asked.

Mrs. Bartle looked pleasantly surprised. "Are you sure, dear? I don't want to bore you with my old-lady rambling down memory lane. Surely your life is too busy for that." Translation: *I know you are lonely, and I shouldn't rub your nose in my happy memories of true love.*

"It's only two o'clock, and my shift doesn't start for eight more hours," Diana said. "I've got tons of time. So go ahead, indulge me with your reminiscing. Maybe it'll give me something to hope for." Diana leaned forward, setting her elbows down on Mrs. Bartle's yellow-and-blue gingham tablecloth as she looked into her friend's dancing blue eyes. Mrs. Bartle's eyes always danced when she was thinking of Henry.

"Well, it was the summer of 1928, and I was eighteen years old," Mrs. Bartle began. "It was a really hot day, so I went over to JP's Drugstore to get a soda—people did that back then. And standing behind the counter was the handsomest young man I had ever seen, dressed all in white. Of course, he had to be." She smiled. "That was his uniform—white slacks, a crisp white buttoned-up shirt, and one of those cute little white hats that all the soda fountain boys used to wear. Well, there was another fellow working with him, and I later found out they flipped a quarter to see which one of them would wait on me." Mrs. Bartle raised her eyebrows at Diana, like she couldn't quite believe it herself.

"You must've been so pretty," Diana said dreamily, trying to imagine finding true love across the counter at Blue Horizon Diner. But, unfortunately, she knew that most of her customers would rather save their quarters for her tip than as a way to compete for her attention. They did that in other ways—like with the rude comments they made about her weight behind her back.

"Oh, I was nothing compared to some of the girls who pined for Henry," Mrs. Bartle answered modestly. "You see, even though he waited on me that day, we were both too shy to do any real talking, but still, I was smitten. So I made a point of going back there every afternoon, except for Tuesdays when I had my piano lesson. And soon I saw I wasn't alone, but that, in fact, I shared the counter with several of his admirers. I never thought he'd choose *me*. My mother wouldn't allow me to wear makeup, you know, and I always felt so plain next to the others. Some of them were quite glamorous."

"Well, why did you keep going back?" Diana asked. "I mean, if you didn't think you stood a chance?"

"Well, I had to go after what I wanted, dear," Mrs. Bartle explained, as if the answer were obvious.

"Oh," Diana said, embarrassed that she wouldn't have done the same thing. "I guess I never wanted anything that badly." She knew this was a lie. She wanted some things very badly, especially love. But she would never risk humiliation to pursue something she'd most likely fail at anyway. It was humiliating enough to tote fifty extra pounds around a bunch of hungry men who blamed cold coffee on the size of their server's ass. Diana realized that Mrs. Bartle must have been thin and that her mother probably wouldn't let her wear makeup because she was afraid the boys would try to take advantage of a girl who was already so pretty without it. She knew it was ridiculous to be jealous of her ninety-three-year-old friend's eighteen-year-old self, but it was impossible for her not to be. She was jealous of anyone who'd ever possessed thinness and beauty. It didn't matter when.

"But then, finally," Mrs. Bartle continued excitedly, "after weeks of smiles and sodas, Henry asked me out for a hamburger."

"And?" Diana asked, leaning in for the steamy details.

"And six months later, we got married." Mrs. Bartle sat back in her chair and raised her happy eyes upward, as if her and Henry's most wonderful moment could be seen playing itself out on the ceiling.

That was one bad thing about old people: they always skipped over the good parts.

CHAPTER THREE

"And would you like rye toast or white?" Diana asked. It was 12:15 a.m. Five hours and forty-five minutes to go until she could hang up her apron and drive to The Doughnut Bin for a large coffee with hazelnut cream and a chocolate banana muffin. That was always the prettiest time of day—the way the morning hung between night and dawn, in a haze of twinkling streetlights singing their swan song against a sleepy pink sun. The ride home would tickle her senses with the enticing *devour-me* aromas of her breakfast, which could never be eaten until she was on her living room couch watching Marsha Douglas forecast the weather during the last ten minutes of the six o'clock news. Marsha's petite stature and chiseled facial features always motivated Diana to skip the next day's muffin and never have another one, to get on some sort of special diet program that would make *her* the kind of woman that fat girls sat on their sofas eating *their* last muffins to. But the motivation was always short-lived. Since she'd been on the night shift, Diana had eaten her last Doughnut Bin muffin six-hundred-and-fourteen times.

"I don't care. Just make it quick," snarled the sweaty-browed man on the other side of the counter.

While she waited for his order to cook, Diana pretended to clean the opposite end of the counter, which, although already spotless, was an unoccupied area of the diner where she could be alone to fantasize about what it would be like to have Mrs. Bartle's luck—to look up one day from the dirty dishtowel she was using to wipe away other people's accidents and literally bump eyes with the man who would spend the rest of his life making her happy, the man who would love her the way no other soul possibly could, the man who would see through her layers of emptiness, boredom and fat and think she was pretty, the man who would never stop to consider that losing weight would make her prettier. With Diana's luck, she *would* meet that man—and he'd die freakishly young, leaving her all alone, just like her father had done.

"Come on, Dee, this ain't a beauty parlor," interrupted Mick, her boss, who had just caught her using the side of the napkin dispenser as a mirror. "Besides, who you got to impress, huh?" he asked, laughing and whacking her on the butt with a roll of quarters as he made his way to the register.

Diana escaped to the kitchen, wondering what it would be like to check her face without worrying that people would question why a woman so fat even bothered to care what was going on above the shoulders. It would be different if she were thin like Brooke, the new nineteen-year-old waitress who'd probably made more in tips in the three weeks she'd worked there than Diana had in the past three months. If Mick had caught Brooke playing beauty parlor in the napkin dispenser, he would have found it charming, and all in attendance would have been subjected to watching a fifty-three-year-old man blush like a teenage girl as he fiddled with a line like *What's a doll like* you *worried about her looks for?*

"Uh, I ordered *white* toast with this," Mr. Sweaty Brow complained as Diana set his plate down.

"Actually, sir, you told me you didn't care as I long as I made it quick, which is *technically* not in my control since I don't cook the food. I just take the orders," Diana explained, putting on her best cute and apologetic face. She liked to practice her cuteness on the really burly and unattractive customers, her theory being that these men were just springboards to bounce coquettish tactics off of, and that since she wasn't actually *interested* in any of them, she had nothing to lose. Apparently this one wasn't biting.

"Yeah, well, then you should learn to take orders correctly," he snapped. "Now either you go get me a couple of slices of *white* bread, or I ask for the manager!"

"Did someone say 'manager'?" Mick asked, rushing to Diana's side.

"Yeah, I asked the lady for white toast, and here she is telling me it ain't her fault that she gave me rye."

With one look from Mick, Diana could tell that although he had rushed immediately to her side, he wouldn't be standing by it.

"Diana, you know we don't argue with our customers," he reprimanded her, taking Mr. Sweaty Brow's plate in his hands. "I'm sorry, sir. We'll fix this right up for ya."

"I wasn't arguing with him, Mick," Diana protested as she followed her boss through the kitchen doors.

"Dee, I *know* that," Mick said, setting down the plate he'd been carrying as he turned to face her. And then he placed his hands firmly on her shoulders, looking her square in the eyes like he was about to teach her one of life's great lessons. "I wanna tell you something," he began. "It's a little saying about business that's always helped me. The customer is always right. Can you say that? Repeat after me. The customer…is always…right."

Diana glared at him, despising the way he talked down to her, especially the way he spoke slowly, like she was some sort of idiot that couldn't process bullshit informtion. "The customer is always right," she muttered through her teeth.

"I can't hear you," Mick taunted.

"I said the customer is always right," she blurted, highly irritated and wishing she were better at hiding it. "Can I take my break now?"

"Yeah, go ahead," Mick conceded. "But there ain't no shortcake left. Try the meringue. It's low fat." Just what

every overweight woman craved: diet tips from her condescending male boss, who had absolutely no place giving
her any because his stomach was bigger than hers was—
and only acceptable, of course, because he was a man.

Diana decided to skip the stale dessert case altogether,
opting for the bag of cheese curls she had in her purse
instead. However, since she was too ashamed to have
anyone know she carried food around in her purse, she
ran over to the Quickmart next door, bought a lottery
ticket so the guy at the counter wouldn't think she'd
come for no reason, and returned with the cheese curls
in hand as if she had just purchased them. Naturally, this
was a time-consuming cover-up, and when she got back,
Mick was already counting down the seconds that remained in her break.

"Eat those up quick. Break's almost over," he said,
loudly enough for the kitchen staff to hear. "Oh, and
make sure you wipe your mouth real good. That pow-
dery orange cheese stuff sometimes sticks to your face.
You don't want to scare away the customers." His laughter echoed in her head with every piece she popped into
her mouth, every bite she took, and every bit she swal-
lowed, leaving her to ponder the question that had to be
on everybody's mind—how it was that a man so god-
damned funny had ended up in the diner business.

CHAPTER FOUR

"I really need to leave, sweetie. Daddy's getting tired from reading all these stories, and he has a long drive ahead of him. Remember, I have to get there before Mommy so I can cook her that surprise anniversary dinner we talked about. You'll be a good little girl while you're here with Mrs. Kingsly, right?"

"Daddy, please don't go. Stay here and read to me some more. Mommy can go to the seashore by herself."

Diana's father laughed adoringly at his six-year-old, strawberry-blond princess, tugging gently on one of her curls until it straightened and then watching it bounce back into place. "Oh, now, I don't think Mommy would like that too much," he said, repeatedly playing with that one single curl until he got her to smile. "We'll spend time together when I get back, okay?"

"Okay," Diana said reluctantly. She wanted to be a big girl and make Daddy proud.

"And I'll read you lots of stories then. And maybe, if you're a really good girl while I'm gone, I'll take you to the zoo."

"When?" Diana asked excitedly, her eyes as wide as saucers.

"When I come home, silly. We'll figure out a special day—for just you and me. But now you have to give Daddy hugs and kisses. It's time to say goodbye."

Diana stood up, tears streaming violently down her cheeks as her father's image waved in and out of sight, growing paler and bolder, paler and bolder, as if flashes of lightning were at the same time illuminating his face and washing it away. "I won't say goodbye! I won't! I won't! I won't!"

Her father stretched out his arms, but they couldn't reach her. "But if you don't say goodbye now, you'll never say it." He was no longer visible—it was only his voice. And his voice was begging her. "Don't you see? This is your last chance. So say it, Diana. Say goodbye. Say it before I fall asleep at the wheel, and my car crashes and bursts into flames and you never see me again."

"NO!"

It was the same dream. Although sometimes the ending was different. Sometimes Diana warned him of what was to come, and he only laughed and tugged at her hair. Other times, like this one, he was the one to warn her. But always, the dream ended in a fiery crash that left his little girl to wonder what love was without him and why she had ever made him so tired in the first place, so tired that he fell asleep driving. And it always left her hating herself—for killing the only person who could ever really make her smile.

CHAPTER FIVE

Through the keyhole, Mrs. Bartle looked like a little white raisin with huge blue eyes. Her eyes always looked big and pleading when she was about to ask a favor, like she was afraid of disturbing the balance of Diana's busy life. The irony there was that Mrs. Bartle had a far more exciting life than Diana had ever had—she at least had happy memories.

"Dear, I was wondering if you could drive me down to the dry cleaners," she said when Diana opened the door. "I would walk, but the man on the news said it's unseasonably hot today and that old fuddy-duddies like me shouldn't be outdoors for long periods of time."

Diana giggled. "Well, you're not an old fuddy-duddy, Mrs. Bartle, but of course I'll take you. Maybe we could stop for lunch on the way back."

"Oh, I'd love to, dear," Mrs. Bartle answered regretfully, "but I've got bridge with the girls at one o'clock."

"Is it Monday already?" Diana asked. "I guess I forgot." Mrs. Bartle had been playing bridge with "the girls" every Monday afternoon since before Henry retired. For more than thirty years, the same ladies had been coming to her place, once the house she shared with Henry and now her apartment, to have tea and cherry strudel and to play cards. All the same ladies except for one—Mrs. Glickman died of liver failure last year. She had been buried on a Monday morning, and they played bridge that same afternoon with one of the other ladies' daughters in her place, explaining that "Esther would have wanted it that way." Mrs. Bartle had since asked Diana to join the group, but Diana had declined. Sitting around a table full of old ladies every Monday afternoon would feel too much like giving up— a public declaration of her inability to form a normal social life. She could only imagine what her mother would say if she found out. *Oh, Diana, really! Can't you find friends your own age?* Besides, it kind of scared her to fill the seat of a dead woman. She didn't want to be the new generation of bridge, especially if meant replacing the old one as its members dropped like flies. It seemed that by becoming Mrs. Glickman's permanent replacement, she'd be admitting that people actually *died* when they died, that fond memories were worthless when there was a game to be played, and that old people weren't built to last. And she didn't want Mrs. Bartle to realize these things. The poor woman had already buried a beloved husband and a cherished lifetime friend. Filling that cherished friend's spot at the bridge table would be like waving a sign: *Out with the old, in with the new!* Diana didn't want to be a symbol of grave mortal realities in the game circle, a constant reminder that replacements would need to be made for Mrs. Bartle's other two friends at some inevitable point in time. Or maybe she was just a coward. Not that she worried much about Mrs. Bartle's life span. That woman was more than alive, and she had enough energy to light the busiest city skyline on the darkest night of the year. And she knew it. She'd often boasted to Diana that the last three generations of women in her family had lived to be at least a hundred-and-one-years old, the youngest to die having been her mother, whose death was purely accidental and could not be attributed to failing health. A very heavy sleeper, as the story went, Mrs. Bartle's mother had dozed off in a lawn chair on an overcast afternoon and had awoken some time later to a turbulent storm already in progress. On her way to seek shelter in the house, she was struck down by a tree that had been hit by a bolt of lightning. Mrs. Bartle's father, who had died one month earlier, had planted the tree, and the family had said that knocking it down was his way of calling his wife home. Then there was her grandmother, who had lived to be a hundred and two, and her great-grandmother, who had died the day before her hundred-and-third birthday. Mrs. Bartle was just a vivacious ninety-three now. A hundred-and-one was still eight years away. And in eight years, Diana would be forty. Who knew if *she'd* live that long? Who knew if she even wanted to?

"You know, dear," Mrs. Bartle said, "you really should try playing with us some time. Mrs. Livingston's niece is interested in learning the game. If you became her part-ner, then we could have tournaments—you know, where one team watches and then plays the winner. That could be fun for everybody, and it would really give both of you a chance to watch the pros in action from time to time."

"Oh, I don't know, Mrs. Bartle. I've got..." Diana didn't want to lie to her. She had no genuine excuse and couldn't bring herself to make one up. Fortunately, Mrs. Bartle always knew when to save her.

"Oh, I understand, dear," she said, waving her little hand to dismiss the idea. "I know how busy you are, doing whatever it is you young people do these days. Just know you're always welcome."

"Thanks," Diana said gratefully. Something she loved about Mrs. Bartle was that she not only included her amongst the youth of the day, but that she also never asked any questions that would reveal what Diana actually did with her afternoons. Not that talk shows were a bad thing. It's just that living for other people's lives can make a thirty-two-year-old woman keenly aware that she needs to find one of her own.

Do you know a woman who is over thirty and thinks she will NEVER get married because her father abandoned her and now she has a weight problem? Are YOU that woman? Well, then you could be a guest on the Jessica Henley Show! Just dial 1-800-JESSICA and tell us your story.

Diana turned off the television and picked up the phone. After a few deep breaths, she allowed her fingers to dial, and with each passing ring, she struggled with the impulse to just hang up. But then somebody answered, and she knew it was too late.

"Hello."

"Hi Mom." There was no turning back now.

"Diana! Are you calling to cancel lunch for Thursday? Because I must tell you, I was thinking of doing the same thing. I've signed up for a new aerobics class, and realizing you probably wouldn't be interested in going with me—I mean, we both know exercise has never really been your thing…" Mrs. Christopher paused to lend a little laugh to her insult, continuing just as Diana was about to interrupt with the real reason she'd called. "Anyway, I'd scheduled the class for Monday and Wednesday afternoons so that we could still keep our lunches. But judging by how tired today's class made me, and since it's the first week and all, I was thinking it would be easier on my body if I used Thursday as kind of a relax day, you know—a little R and R for my muscles, which I must admit are not used to all the work!"

"Mom?" Diana could feel her nerve waning. It was now or never.

"Oh, honey, I'm not talking about every Thursday, just this first one."

"Mom?"

"I mean, it's not like we'd be stopping the weekly lunch thing altogether. Hey, I'll tell ya what. How about we switch Ping's to Fridays? I mean, you're not busy on Fridays are you?"

"Mom?"

"Well, are you, Diana?"

"Mom?"

"Yes, honey, what's the matter? You've hardly said a thing!"

Diana counted silently to five, her head spinning, her heart pounding. This was one of the scariest and most embarrassing things she ever had to admit, but she couldn't keep it to herself another day. She needed her mother's help. "Mom," she began, her voice wavering, "I'm pregnant."

CHAPTER SIX

Diana sat uncomfortably on the plastic table. Dr. Mason and her mother were peering at her like she was some sort of dead insect they were viewing through a microscope—their faces revealed pity, intrigue and something that vaguely resembled disgust.

"You see, Diana," Dr. Mason explained, "immaculate conceptions have become increasingly rare in the past two thousand years." Diana was too embarrassed to roll her eyes, even though Dr. Mason, the gynecologist she'd shared with her mother since she was seventeen, and normally a kind man, suddenly reminded her of Mick—just another frustrated comedian in the wrong line of work. Then again, how could she expect him to take her seriously after her mother laughingly introduced her ailment as "ghost impregnation," explaining that although

Diana had not had sex since high school, she actually *believed* herself to be pregnant? The truth was that Diana had no idea what was going on. She'd been too mortified to buy a home pregnancy test. But pregnancy was the only explanation she could think of for two months of missed periods.

"Dr. Mason," Mrs. Christopher interjected, "do you think there's a chance that she—now, Diana, don't get upset with me for saying this—but do you think that maybe Diana wanted to get pregnant so badly that she sort of willed her body into a false pregnancy? You hear about that sort of thing every now and again, don't you?"

Diana shot an angry glance at her mother. She now knew what it was like to have violent thoughts toward others. She'd been having them toward herself for longer than she cared to remember, but having them toward someone else, though in a sense liberating, was also infuriating. How dare her mother presume to know *anything* about her private dreams and hallucinations? And how dare she speak before a third party when her presumptions were so ridiculously off base? Diana didn't want a baby.

"Diana, your mother is right," Dr. Mason said. "Many times, women who want children so desperately can actually create the physical symptoms of pregnancy for themselves. These women usually think they have miscarried when they get their periods, so they end up going to the doctor who then informs them that they were never really pregnant to begin with."

"But, Dr. Mason," Diana said, opening her mouth for

the first time since she'd gotten there, "I don't *want* a baby. Look, all I know is that I've gotten my period on schedule every single month since I was twelve, and last month, I didn't get it at all. And this month, I'm already ten days late."

"Diana, do you have a secret boyfriend?" Mrs. Christopher asked, her patronizing eyes glittering wildly at the prospect of her daughter actually having a life.

Dr. Mason's face grew serious. It seemed he'd gotten so caught up in the humor he and her mother appeared to find in all of this that he'd overlooked a grave possibility that was only now occurring to him. "What Diana may have, Patty, is some sort of cyst or tumor in her fallopian tube that is inhibiting her menstrual cycle."

Tumor? Diana was horrified. She had often thought about death, many times considering it a welcome alternative to bumbling through life, but now that it was practically staring her in the face, she suddenly realized that her death wish needed to be refined to include catastrophic accidents only—like the kind that had killed her father—not some terrible disease that would eat away at her for months. To die of cancer would be worse than dealing with her weight and her mother and Mick *and* those hungry, insulting truckers for the rest of her life. A terrible diagnosis like that would *welcome* living. And what would Diana do with a will to live when her only real motivation to even *exist* was knowing that one day these loathsome daily struggles that defined her would meet their end?

"In most cases, these tumors are benign," Dr. Mason continued.

"But what about Diana's weight gain?" Mrs. Christopher asked quickly, the color rushing back to her face, which had turned a ghastly white upon the sound of the word *tumor.* "I mean is pregnancy a total impossibility?" Funny how her mother, who had practically laughed her into the next time zone when Diana confessed that she might be pregnant, now seemed to think that immaculate conception was more believable than cancer.

"Well, Diana has *been* gaining weight pretty steadily since I've known her," Dr. Mason said, seemingly insistent on kicking Diana while she was down. "And if she has not had sexual intercourse in as long as she tells us she hasn't..." Kick number two. "Well, then I think we'd better do an ultrasound and find out just what it is we're dealing with here."

"And what happens if you find something?" Mrs. Christopher asked, beginning to appear numb.

"Well, in that case, I'd have to say that the best thing to do would be to schedule an immediate biopsy," Dr. Mason paused, responding to the desperate look in Mrs. Christopher's eyes. Diana had already begun to feel indifferent. And it annoyed her that Dr. Mason was playing more to her mother's emotions than to her own when *she* was clearly the wounded party. "We can do the ultrasound right now."

It's funny how much one's life can change in such a short period of time. Or maybe it's too serious to be funny. Maybe it's ironic. While Dr. Mason flipped through his date book, Diana wrestled for the adjective—for just the right adjective to describe how one minute her mother and gynecologist could be ridiculing her to shreds for being an undersexed fatty, and the next, they could be planning the details of her biopsy. "I have a breakfast I can cancel…" Dr. Mason muttered to himself. "Is tomorrow at 8:00 a.m. good for you?"

"It's fine," Diana said, choking back her own breakfast and wondering how many more chocolate banana muffins she'd be able to eat and feel guilty about before she died.

CHAPTER SEVEN

"I had a lump in my breast once," Mrs. Bartle said, setting a plate of peanut butter cookies down on the table.

"You did?" Diana asked, hoping to hear one of those little, happy-ending stories that Mrs. Bartle was so famous for. The scene at Dr. Mason's that morning had replayed itself over and over in her mind until all of their voices were in slow motion. She really needed to press Pause for a while.

"Take a cookie, dear. I just baked them this morning."

This was the first time Diana could ever remember *not* fighting the urge to devour a plate of cookies in Mrs. Bartle's kitchen. But she didn't want to hurt her friend's feelings, so she selected one and watched it tremble in her hand as she waited for the burning, nauseous sensation in her stomach to give way to appetite. And then she saw the concern in Mrs. Bartle's eyes and forced herself to try a small piece. "Tell me about the lump," she said, quickly realizing just how damn good freshly baked peanut butter cookies were—even to someone who had just received a death sentence. They truly were a cookie for all occasions. She took another one.

"Well, I was fifty-three years old, and I was terrified," Mrs. Bartle said. "But the doctor removed it, and it turned out to be benign, as I'm sure this cyst or tumor will be in your case, dear."

There was that word again—*tumor*. It was such an ugly word, uglier than fat, uglier than loneliness, uglier than a thirty-two-year-old woman who hadn't had sex since high school. Diana wanted to change the subject and ask Mrs. Bartle what sex was like when two people were in love. But for as many things as she could talk to her friend about, she could not talk to this ninety-three-year-old woman, however hip and lively and amazingly liberal she was for her age, about sex. Actually, she didn't feel much like talking at all. She just didn't want to be alone. That was one of the many great things about having a friend like Mrs. Bartle. She understood Diana in these quiet and reflective moments—she had them, too. It was an unspoken, but very sacred law between the two women never to ask what the other was thinking about at these times, but just to remain silent, sipping tea and nibbling on cookies, each leaving the other to her private meditations. Sometimes during these pensive periods, Mrs. Bartle's magnificent blue eyes would rise from their cradle of age spots and wrinkles to meet with

Diana's, and the old woman would take a shortcut into a secret world where happiness was seldom and self-torment exhausted itself in an endlessly steady supply. Mrs. Bartle was the only visitor Diana would permit to enter this world—she was the only one with a pass. Diana allowed her to have it because she liked their connection; in fact, she treasured it—especially in light of her theory that if someone as exceptionally functional as Mrs. Bartle could understand and appreciate the screwed-up world inside of her, then she couldn't possibly be as out of touch with inner normalcy as she thought. However, right now Diana really hoped her gracious mentor *wouldn't* link eyes with her and commiserate with the debilitating plight of her lonely existence. This was because she was thinking about Barry, and thoughts of Barry were tremendously private.

Barry was the guy who took Diana's virginity in high school. He didn't exactly *take* it—she gave it to him. And thank God she did, or else she wouldn't be a thirty-two-year-old woman who hadn't had sex since high school—she'd be a thirty-two-year-old *virgin,* which would be even creepier. Diana gave herself to Barry when she was seventeen, in the back of his powder blue pickup truck at a neighbor's New Year's Eve party. It wasn't a high school party, but was actually at the house of a family that Diana had done some baby-sitting for during her freshman and sophomore years. Even though Diana was a senior at the time, and no longer the Suttons' regular Saturday-night sitter, Mrs. Sutton had invited her to the party so she could look after the kids while she and her husband pretended not to have any. Apparently, the thirteen-year-old who normally watched them had plans already. Diana wasn't technically a guest, but she was permitted to have fun as long as she kept an eye on Sarah and Jack and made sure they didn't bother anybody. Aside from the Suttons' nine-year-old twins, Diana was the youngest one at the party. She'd planned on leaving after she put the kids to bed, but upon hearing that she had no other parties to rush off to, Mrs. Sutton had invited her to stay, which was when she officially became a guest. And as a guest, she began talking to Barry, the Suttons' mechanic and family friend. She'd noticed him looking at her throughout the night—while she was braiding Sarah's hair, while she was cleaning up a spilled glass of chardonnay, and when, on numerous occasions, she was caught staring at *him* from across the room while the adults fawned over the twins, leaving her awkward and alone with nothing else to do. Once she was done working, she noticed that not only was this a man who noticed her but that this was also a man with the deepest brown eyes and the warmest and sexiest grin she had ever seen. She'd overheard one of the guests teasing him about only being twenty-eight and therefore too young to listen to the dirty joke being told, which still made him eleven whole years older than Diana, but she didn't mind. All the guys her own age at school were immature anyway and wouldn't have given her the time of day even if she'd asked for it. Barry was different. By the way he kept looking at her, she could tell he didn't care about shallow things like whether or not she was thin. The fact that

he saw through the surface, which was more than anyone else had ever bothered to see, meant that without ex-
changing a single word, he already understood her better
than anyone else ever had.

After nearly an hour of glances and coy smiles, Diana
had promised herself that the next time she and Barry
made eye contact, she would approach him. The promise had driven her into the bathroom, where she'd stared
at herself in the mirror, racking her brains for some last
minute trick that would make her appear twenty pounds
thinner. When she came out, Barry was standing in the
hallway, just a few feet from the door. They approached
each other simultaneously, both saying "hi" at the exact
same time, which spawned laughter on both sides—a
perfectly scripted icebreaker if ever there was one.

"Let's start over," he had said, leaning one hand against
the wall just above Diana's head, and placing his other
hand on the woodwork beside her waist. "Hi, I'm Barry."

"Hi Barry," she'd said, lifting her eyes to meet the gaze
of the handsome older stranger who'd just trapped her
with his territorial stance.

"You're Diana, right?"

"How did you know my name?" Diana had asked,
wondering if her breath smelled. She hadn't been that
close to a boy since Billy Jackson had kissed her in his
tree house when they were ten, which had only lasted
eight seconds and had only happened at all because one
of their other friends had bet Billy three packs of gum
that he couldn't go through with it. This was very different, very romantic…and *very* adult.

"I've done my homework," Barry had answered. "I've been asking about you."

"You have?"

"I sure have," he'd said, showing off that million-dollar grin again. "You wanna take a walk outside with me for a minute?"

"I hope it's more than a minute," she had teased, having absolutely no idea where the remark had come from and what she was getting herself into—while at the same time having *every* idea and not being afraid.

"I like the way you think," he said with a laugh, putting his hand on her back as he let her lead the way to the Suttons' front door.

The air outside smelled like leftover snow and the full, frosty moon was so beautiful it looked fake. Something big was about to happen. Maybe it was the full moon or the freshness of the cold during those first minutes of 1988, or maybe it was just her, but she knew something was about to change and she was ready.

Barry took her to his truck and immediately leaned her against the passenger side door, not even pausing to notice her reaction before he began kissing her—with an eagerness and intensity Diana had only seen directed at size-six actresses in the movies. But before she could even comprehend the magnitude of the moment, they'd moved on to another one, and Barry was guiding her to the back of the pickup, where she could see there was a blanket already laid out. The major embarrassment came when she realized he was trying to lift her but couldn't. So to salvage the moment, she'd climbed in herself, stepping onto one of the truck's rear tires while Barry helped her along, pushing her in by way of her *own* rear tire and climbing in right behind her. Diana lay down on the blanket as Barry settled on top of her, unbuttoning her blue-and-white-checked flannel shirt as he kissed his way down her neck. Diana prayed she looked sexy enough in her white cotton discount store sports bra, although she really wished she was wearing something more vixen-like, like one of those black lacy numbers worn by the perfect-breasted women in her mother's mail-order lingerie catalogs. When Barry began unzipping his pants, Diana figured she should do the same, remembering as she reached for her jeans button that she wasn't wearing good underwear either. Not that she owned any. Diana's drawer was forever stocked with the big, comfortable, cotton ones that women like her mother owned just one or two pair of and only wore when it was "that time of the month." But unlike these women, Diana didn't feel she could afford to be picky for those other three weeks when life was less cruel, and besides, sexy underwear didn't even come in her size. Not that she knew this for a fact or anything, because if it did come in her size, she'd have been too mortified to go shopping for it anyway. Regardless, it didn't matter in this case: Barry seemed to be completely unaffected by her choice of underwear. Maybe it was because he never saw them. Diana had experienced so much difficulty trying to shimmy gracefully out of her pants that when they'd gotten stuck around the bottom of her butt, she'd just left them there, and Barry had yanked them down, her underwear included, the rest of the way to her knees, where they'd remained for the duration of the act. It had all happened so quickly—the stares, the smiles, the cold, the moon, the warmth, the kisses, the nakedness. And then there was a sharp, penetrating pain.

Diana had tried not to scream. And when the hot blood began to trickle down her inner thighs, she'd tried not to faint. It didn't feel very good physically, but emotionally, she felt like she'd just been given a free year's supply of self-esteem. She had never been so desired by, or so close to, a man. And that part felt terrific. As for the hips down, she went numb after a while, and while Barry continued on top of her, she allowed her eyes to fixate on the glorious stars that had crowned this monumental rite of passage into womanhood.

Barry finished his business on Diana's stomach and collapsed onto her chest, which had made her feel masculine because in the movies, it was always the woman cuddling on the *man's* chest. Not that she and Barry had really cuddled afterward. It was more like he just lay there like a vegetable for a couple of minutes before standing up abruptly, hopping out of the truck, and walking around to the glove compartment. He came back with a wad of tissues.

"Here," he'd said awkwardly, his eyes as guilty as a naughty child's, "you can…" He didn't say the words. Perhaps he couldn't—he seemed so flustered. All he did was make a wiping motion in the direction of her stomach, clear his throat, and say "here" again as he handed Diana the tissues.

"Thanks," she'd said, watching Barry as he stood there trying *not* to watch her, scratching his face nervously and sniffing a lot. Every once in a while he'd steal a sideways glance at her, perhaps to see if she was done cleaning herself off yet. Diana didn't feel awkward at all. She was too busy wondering if anyone had seen her leave the party and marveling over the fact that she had just done it—finally! She was elated, and glowing in a way she'd only read about. When she was done with the tissues, she'd reached out her hand for Barry to help her down from the truck but had to clear her throat loudly when she realized he couldn't see her—he was still avoiding eye contact.

Once they were both on equal ground, there was one moment, one brief yet forever-to-be-remembered moment, in which Barry's eyes met hers—and they looked terrified. Diana couldn't figure out what he could be so scared of, but then again, since the reality of sex was so different than anything she'd ever seen or imagined, maybe all guys got that terrified look in their eyes afterward and no one ever talked about it. *She* certainly didn't plan to. Just because they'd just had sex didn't mean they had to start talking about their inner feelings. Besides, Barry looked like he was in more of a hurry to get out of there than he'd been to actually get *out* there. And Diana was in a hurry to begin replaying every single detail of what they'd just done over and over again until it became a permanent fixture in her brain.

"Why don't you get back inside before you catch a chill," he'd said, breaking the silence and patting her lightly on the shoulder, like after all that, it was the only physical intimacy he could muster, which wasn't offensive, just ironic.

"Okay," she'd agreed, smiling lightly as Barry gave her one last quick shoulder pat to remember him by and walked around to the other side of the truck. He drove away a few seconds later, and Diana never saw him again. And that was the first and last time she'd ever had sex.

She spilled the news to her mother over New Year's Day salads during some local parade on the community cable station. She hadn't intended to tell her, but the memory was still shooting butterflies through her stomach and Mrs. Christopher kept insisting she say what was on her mind. She wasn't used to seeing Diana so happy— especially not during bland diet lunches and good-natured programming. The teenage daughter *she* knew was into junk food and trash TV—this bright, sunny attitude was extremely out of line. She worried that Diana had gotten her hands on some kind of weight loss amphetamines and the speed had gone straight to her brain. After some prodding, Diana finally admitted that she was sorry to burst her mother's bubble—she wasn't on a diet—but that she was extremely happy because she'd met a man at the Suttons' party. And, yes, by "man," she meant older. And, yes, they did have sex. Of course, Mrs. Christopher did not share in Diana's jubilation. In fact, she'd staunchly disapproved, forcing Diana to spend an entire day at the free clinic testing for pregnancy and diseases because she was too embarrassed for Dr. Mason to know that her daughter had been "loose." Diana didn't really know much about AIDS then, but looking back now, she could see why her mother was so upset that she'd had unprotected sex with a stranger—information she hadn't volunteered when she'd told her about Barry, but had been forced to admit when asked if he'd worn a condom, which was a question she hadn't expected and, since she was terrible at lying on the spot, was also a question her mother had known the answer to before Diana could even think to make one up. But after all the tests came back negative, it was no longer the fact that she'd risked her health and safety that Mrs. Christopher so harshly objected to, but the fact that Barry was so much older and that Diana had essentially acted like one of those women that every girl's mother warns her not to become—a slut. And *this* was the disapproval that had gotten Diana through so many of life's boring moments, which there never seemed to be a shortage of during her teenage years. For months, even when the most exciting event in her day was dessert, she was able to walk around like she had a life. And better yet, a *romantic* life that her mother resented. Many lonely walks home from school and countless sleepless nights were passed fantasizing about similar opportunities she might have to incur her mother's disapproval in the future. But unfortunately, most men she met with were not as desperate as Barry, and the only way Diana would ever manage to provoke her mother's disapproval again, besides with her weight, was in her *not* being able to find a man *since* she lost her virginity at age seventeen.

***

"Would you like some more cookies, dear?" The sweet sound of Mrs. Bartle's voice pulled Diana away from the memory of the one passionate thing that had ever happened to her and drew her attention to the embarrassing reality that thinking about sex had caused her to unknowingly devour an entire plate of peanut butter cookies. She wondered if Mrs. Bartle had even gotten a chance to eat *one*.

"Okay."

As her friend headed to the pantry, Diana made a promise to herself. *If I kick this cancer thing*, she vowed, *I WILL have sex again…and it won't be in the back of a pickup truck this time.*

CHAPTER EIGHT

"Hey, uh, what are ya, still sleepin'?" Mick asked loudly, poking anxiously at Diana's shoulder like she was some sort of stoned zombie that couldn't hear unless manhandled. "Your order's up. Oh, and by the way, you don't get paid to daydream."

Mick the dick. Not even he could spoil her mood. Not Mick. Not Brooke, the diner goddess, whose looks in her direction always said, *I hope I'm not still working here when I'm in MY thirties, and I really hope I don't ever look like THAT.* Not even the crabby customers and the likes of Mr. Sweaty Brow could destroy the overwhelming sense of peace she'd attained in her sleep that afternoon.

When she'd gotten into bed, her stomach full of peanut butter cookies from Mrs. Bartle's kitchen, she was more exhausted than she could remember being in a long time, so exhausted in fact that she didn't have any time to worry about the coming morning's hospital visit, for she was almost fast asleep before her head even hit the pillow. And while she slept, she dreamt of a garden—a radiant and ravishing one full of beautiful, vibrant, and brilliantly pink azaleas at the peak of their bloom. And she stood in the middle of it, staring up at a sky as blue as every ocean should be, and wondering how it was possible that such breathtaking perfection had ever escaped her eye in the past. For this was her garden, her sky, the only home she had ever known. But it had never looked so beautiful. And she had never been so at peace or so in love with the world. The air, the flowers, everything smelled sweeter and felt better than anything she could think to compare it to. And from out of the clouds came a blimp. It said R…O… The painted black letters emerged slowly, becoming less obscured by the clouds and more enlightened by the sun as the blimp sailed smoothly across the sky…M… Something descended from underneath of it, a ladder…U… It was a shiny gold rope ladder and onto it stepped a man…T… It was her father. And there were no more letters coming. She'd been reading them backwards anyway. The blimp above her garden said TUMOR.

Daddy pointed at the flowers, and his smile was sad. Diana was afraid he didn't like them. But when he pointed to himself and then at the flowers again, she realized that he wanted some, and so she motioned to him that it was okay to come closer. But he didn't want to, or maybe he couldn't. And all he did was point—from Diana to the flowers and from the flowers to himself. It seemed he wanted his little, strawberry-curled princess to pick the azaleas for him. And so she gathered up as many of the magical flowers as her two hands could hold and stood on her tiptoes, stretching her arms as far toward the sky as they would go. Gratefully accepting the azalea bouquet and offering her his hand to hold, her father helped her onto the ladder that dangled just a few feet above the brilliant pink petals she'd stood on just moments before. And as they flew away together, leaving behind the only home she had ever known and the only beauty she had ever seen, Diana knew something better awaited her, something beyond the clouds in a place where Daddy would always be. And knowing that filled her with peace, one greater than the garden could ever give her—and one that remained with her even after she awoke.

And now that she was at work, with only eight-and-a-half hours to go until the biopsy that would sentence her to a life in heaven with her father, a life away from all the disappointments she'd known since he'd left her— *including* this job—nothing else mattered but the dream. And Mick's demeaning sarcasm couldn't demean and Brooke's judgmental stares couldn't convict because *this* world meant nothing. Nothing mattered and nothing could break her heart. And soon enough she would be in a better place where Daddy could never leave her again. Just as Mrs. Bartle's father had sent lightning through trees to bring his wife home, Diana's father had given her a tumor the size of a blimp so that he could reunite with *his* angel on earth.

CHAPTER NINE

"Mom, I just want you to know that I'm okay, so don't worry," Diana said as they drove to the hospital. Mrs. Christopher seemed to be having trouble keeping her eyes on the road and had been turning her head every two seconds since Diana entered the car to cast terrified glances of urgency her daughter's way—as if Diana were already dead.

"Oh, honey, I know that," her mother said, grabbing Diana's hand. It was the first time they'd made physical contact in as long as Diana could remember, aside from the accidental bumping of fingers that occasionally occurred when her mother slipped her money for fat clothes. Although it was surely intended as comforting, her mother's touch was as ice cold as it always seemed it would be. Diana smiled to herself, remembering a conclusion she'd come to as a little girl when she'd reasoned, very logically she'd believed, that the explanation for her mother's apparent lack of humanity could be traced to aliens having snatched her soul the year that Daddy died, using it to learn about earthlings as they planned their takeover of the world, and, meanwhile, allowing some totally bitchy and condescending alien to invade her mother's body in order to learn more about the daily routines on Planet Earth. But Diana's amused recollection of childhood theories was dampened when she suddenly noticed how badly the alien driver she called "Mom" was trembling. She realized her mother didn't know she was okay. But that was because she and her mother had very different ideas of what "okay" actually meant. She knew that to her mother, okay meant healthy—in a physical sense, meaning cancer-free, and eventually thin with a better job and, perhaps one day, a husband, whom Diana could not possibly find *until* she was, indeed, thin with a better job. But for Diana, okay was being with someone who loved her in a place where size and occupation had no bearing on how people were perceived. She was so thankful that God had finally heard her prayers.

Diana spent the rest of the ride trying to remember all of the times she had questioned or cursed God's plan, and asking for forgiveness on every count. But the process of finding religion on the way to her biopsy, however inspiring and spiritually cleansing, was still somewhat tainted by the guilt she felt toward a certain panic-stricken woman sitting beside her, a woman who had given birth to something that wanted so badly to die. But when they arrived at the hospital doors, the whole God–Mom–Guilt complex was resolved. Actually, it was more like forgotten, and replaced by a force that was worlds more powerful than both maternal instinct *and* God—Cedar Groves Medical Center, the place that would confirm, and most likely house, her release from the shackles of everything painful and mundane she had ever known. And as she stepped off of the elevator and onto the oncology floor, she could feel her father's unconditional love blooming from within her fallopian tube like beautiful springtime azaleas. Diana couldn't wait to see him…his little girl was coming home.

CHAPTER TEN

Is there a word uglier than *tumor?* There is when the word before it is "benign" and one has spent the last twenty-two hours and twenty-six years wanting to go home.

When Diana hung up with Dr. Mason, she could feel the color draining from her face. She was nauseated, dizzy, paralyzed. She knew she should call her mother but just couldn't bolster the spirit to feign happiness over her "health." And what was health without happiness anyway? Was it healthy to wish the doctors were wrong? Was it healthy to expect that the one living person who was supposed to love her most would undoubtedly use her escape from death as a lesson on the necessity of weight loss? Was it *unhealthy* that she'd rather die than hear it?

That dream in the garden had given her something to

hope for and something to hold on to while she was hop-ing. Unlike her hopes of one day possessing a Meteorol-ogist Marsha Douglas body, she was actually on the road to attaining *this* wish. She hadn't had something to hope for and a reason to think it would happen since Barry and the wild sex streak that was going to bolster her ego while tipping her mother's scales of sanity toward "wacko." But that hadn't been about love or freedom. It had been about insecurity and revenge. This, however, *this* had been about peace *and* love *and* freedom. It had been about happiness. Sure, there would have been a few months of physical an-guish, but that was to have been her earthly repentance— for being fat during most of her living years, for cursing God when those living years were less than a blast, for disappointing her mother, and for never really appreciat-ing the invisible gifts that gracious people were supposed to recognize in their everyday lives and feel blessed for. And that repentance would have *made* her gracious. She was all set to become a pious person—all she'd needed was the disease. She'd been banking on cancer as her ticket to heaven. So, now what? Was heaven really that exclusive? Was the father of the *world* really so eager to keep Diana away from her own? She could feel herself beginning to hate God for rejecting her, and she could even feel His rejection, ringing in her ears—high-pitched, evenly timed, and constant—until her own voice sounded from out of nowhere, putting an end to God's wrath as it told Him to wait for the beep.

Mrs. Christopher spoke loudly onto the answering machine, as if Diana's one-bedroom apartment were so mansion-esque that if she *were* home and just not picking up, the message would go unheard unless shouted. "Diana, it's Mom! Are you there? Diana, I'm assuming you're there. If you are, would you pick up, please?... Oh, where could you be?... Maybe you're with that old lady upstairs again, Mrs., uh, Barton—"

"Bartle," Diana said, picking up the phone to correct her. "And it's downstairs." It was insulting that her mother never remembered Mrs. Bartle's name or what floor she lived on, especially since "that old lady" had only been Diana's only friend for the past three years. It wasn't as if Mrs. Christopher had any *other* names to remember.

"Oh, you're there!" her mother blared with dramatic relief.

"Yeah, Mom, but hold on. We need to stop talking so the machine will go off." Even though the walk to turn off the answering machine was only a few feet away, Diana didn't have the energy to even *think* that this would be a long enough conversation to make that walk worthwhile. And, of course, Mrs. Christopher did not stop talking, so Diana was forced to deal with hearing her mother's echoing voice in both ears.

"What did Dr. Mason say?" Mrs. Christopher continued. "Are you all right? Did he call you yet?"

"Yeah, he called."

"AND?"

"And..." Diana knew she should relish this moment, for it was probably the last time she'd ever have power over her mother, the last time her mother's "motherly concern" would be about something other than her weight and lack of social life. But she had to tell her. "I don't have cancer."

A serenade of *Oh-thank-goodness!*'s and *You-have-no-idea-how-glad-I-am-to-hear-that!*'s followed. But after all forty-two seconds' worth of her mother's jubilance subsided, she felt the need to point out *the lesson-to-be-learned-from-all-of-this*. Diana had known it was coming. After all, all roads led to the almighty diet discussion.

"Now, dear, I must say this cancer scare has been a bit of a blessing in disguise," Mrs. Christopher began. "It's caused you to realize the importance of your health and of taking care of your body. Consider this a fresh start, like today is the first day of the rest of your life." Mrs. Christopher giggled, impressed by what she obviously considered to be a brilliant allusion to their last lunch together, as if remembering the cliché proverb in her daughter's fortune cookie actually meant they were close. "I mean seriously, Diana, you truly *have* been given a second chance at life. It's time to take a serious look at the choices you make. Because, I tell you, it's your everyday choices—the ones you probably think the least about — that actually define who you are. Diana, it's really time for you to start taking care of *you*." Translation: *Now that you don't have cancer, I can start nagging you about your weight again, you big, fat disappointment.* And lucky Diana: since her mother could not manage to shut up for even ten seconds so that the answering machine could stop recording them, she got to hear the entire lecture in stereo.

CHAPTER ELEVEN

"It's benign, Mrs. Bartle," Diana said when she opened the door. Although her friend hadn't asked yet, Diana knew that's what she had come to find out. But Mrs. Bartle's response was very different from what Diana had imagined, completely unlike the "normal" reaction of her mother. She didn't smile. She didn't exhale like she'd been holding her breath ever since she'd first heard the word *tumor*. And she didn't thank God. All she did was stare at Diana with her large, penetrating blue eyes—the eyes that had always seen more than Diana could ever tell—in silence.

Diana looked at the floor. She sensed that Mrs. Bartle knew this wasn't good news, and it shamed her—so much that she began to wish she'd never dreamt of azaleas. If she had never had that vision of her father in the garden, then maybe she'd be glad that life had bitten her in the ass and given her that proverbial second chance. But as things were, she had no will to embrace it. All she wanted now was a reason to break the silence.

"Why don't you come in?" Diana invited. But Mrs. Bartle didn't move. She just stood there and stared, almost blankly. "Mrs. Bartle, are you okay?"

Mrs. Bartle's lower lip began to tremble and she seemed to fall out of her trance. "Diana," she said, looking into her friend's eyes as the tears began to spill from her own, "I miss Henry."

What was this? In the three years that Diana had known Mrs. Bartle, she'd never seen her get sad over Henry. In fact, it had always been just the opposite— Henry was her greatest thrill, her proudest treasure. It was apparent in the wonderful gleam that overtook her eyes whenever his name was mentioned. And even when *no one* said the name Henry, if Mrs. Bartle's eyes happened to glimmer, dance, dream or smile, Diana would know that her friend was in a brilliant place, a place that she, herself, had never personally been since she was probably the only grown woman on the planet who had never been in love. Mrs. Bartle had always seemed so grateful and content with the memories that Diana had never really stopped to think that in her private moments, she had to at least sometimes get sad that Henry wasn't physically around. For memories couldn't hold a woman; they couldn't whisper "I love you" while she slept. Diana scorned herself for having been such a clueless jerk.

This whole time, she'd envied Mrs. Bartle for the lifetime of true love that she'd had. But hadn't the word *had* ever penetrated far enough into Diana's brain to register any meaning? *Had* meant lost, as in "gone," "no more" and "never again." He *had* a turtle. She *had* a job. We *had* a house. Well, Mrs. Bartle *had* a husband. And she'd loved him in a way that she could never love any other human being again, in a way that was deeper and truer and more magical than any fictional romance classic Diana had ever read or seen. But it hadn't been a *lifetime* of true love because Henry was dead. Dead, dead, dead. Dead like Diana's father was dead. And happy memories of Daddy were shit compared to actually *having* a father. How could Diana have failed to realize that when it came to Mrs. Bartle and Henry? She should've known better than anyone how easy it was to mask pain. How could she have been so insensitive?

Diana couldn't find the words to make things better. She didn't even know what "better" was. All she knew was that her best friend was crying, and so she pulled her close, and the two women stood in the doorway hugging for a very long time. Diana's heart was so broken for Mrs. Bartle that the moments passed without distinction in an embrace that seemed to last both forever and not nearly long enough. There were tears, and there was silence. There was stillness, and there was trembling. And then, somehow, there was tea. They sat sipping it once calmness and perception of time had been restored, but Diana only faintly remembered making it. She must have managed to boil the water at some point during that haze of emotional overload, but she was too tired to wonder how and too overcome with the relief that so often follows such dramatic outbursts to care. All she cared about now was Mrs. Bartle and letting her talk about whatever it was that had triggered these feelings about Henry. Maybe talking about it would make her feel less alone. It seemed like a novel concept—actually being *open* about what made life so sad. Diana had never attempted it personally, but it always seemed to work on TV sitcoms. Perhaps if it worked for her friend, Diana might even try the honesty approach herself sometime. But at this moment, she cared light-years more about Mrs. Bartle's stability than she did her own. Maybe because she couldn't recall a single moment in her life when she'd actually *been* stable, so she didn't really know what she was missing out on. Mrs. Bartle, on the other hand, never broke down like this. She was always the pillar of strength in their friendship, the one who never needed any consolation at all—until now, when she suddenly seemed to need a lot.

"Mrs. Bartle, I've watched you talk about Henry tons of times over the past three years, and I've never seen you get sad over him."

"That's because thinking about Henry makes me so happy," Mrs. Bartle said, smiling softly. "It gives me hope for when we will be together again." Diana could relate to that. But only since the garden dream. Before that, thoughts of her father hadn't given her happiness *or* hope. Those things were exceptionally hard to find when every sweet memory ended in a fatal explosion.

"So, why are you so sad today?" Diana asked, refusing to dwell on the fact that her biopsy results had pretty

much destroyed the short-lived hope she'd had of re-
uniting with *her* dearly departed. She couldn't pity herself now, not when Mrs. Bartle needed her.

"Because today is ten years since he died," Mrs. Bartle
said slowly, as if she were testing the truth of something
she still couldn't believe.

"Oh, Mrs. Bartle, I'm so sorry."

"I'm not, dear. Well, I'm sorry he's gone. But he's waiting in a better place for me. And I know we won't be apart
much longer."

Her words sent chills through Diana's entire apartment, punching her in the heart with how harsh and
wrong they were. How could Mrs. Bartle say something
like that? She wasn't at death's door—she was far from it.
This woman was more alive than anyone Diana had ever
known. How could she just give up on what she'd been
so obviously blessed with? God had drenched this woman
with enough extra vitality to feed the lifeless for a lifetime. How could she be so cavalier about that kind of
generosity? How could she even think of denying her
God-given gifts?

"I don't know about that, Mrs. Bartle. You've got a lot
of life in you yet," Diana said, trying not to cry at the
thought of losing her best and only friend, and knowing
that what she was really doing was begging Mrs. Bartle
to keep on living.

Mrs. Bartle took Diana's hand and pressed it firmly in
her own, and looking sternly into her young friend's eyes,
she softly spoke the words, "So do *you*." And that was all
that needed to be said. For afterward, Mrs. Bartle turned

back to her tea and her private reflections of Henry, with a sneaky little smile that showed she knew that, although they would never discuss it, she had just changed Diana's life.

But how had she gotten so wise? How could she have known that Diana had prayed for malignancy and that those prayers had given her hope? How did she take a woman with a death wish and manage to make her realize the irony of her own livelihood? For in that instant, in that one singular moment when Mrs. Bartle began to deny hers, when that total epitome of all that was life seemed to welcome her impending death—a death she claimed wouldn't take much longer to find her—Diana came alive. For the first time, she had fight to argue with and insight to provide: a person could not just go around thinking herself as good as dead when she was still alive, especially when she was so alive, and so young. Mrs. Bartle was only ninety-three. And this meant that Diana was very young—young enough to start over, too young to want to die. She and Mrs. Bartle were both young enough to be *alive*. And alive meant *living*, not constantly looking for your ticket out of it. Alive wasn't being in a hurry to reunite with people who loved you...once. Alive was about right *now*. Diana loved Mrs. Bartle, and she knew that lady was meant to live. Apparently Mrs. Bartle felt the same way about Diana. And if Mrs. Bartle believed it with as much heart as she seemed to, with as much heart as Diana believed it about her, then it had to be true. Life was not about trees getting struck by lightning and tumor blimp reunions in the clouds. It was about living with

what you were given and making the best from whatever you had. And what Diana and Mrs. Bartle had was
their health and each other. It wasn't until Mrs. Bartle, a
woman who had always counted her blessings, seemed
to forget them all that Diana had to step in and come to
her rescue by reminding her of something that she, herself, had never thought she knew—they were both full
of life. Leave it to Mrs. Bartle to make Diana's rescuing
words an apocalypse.

CHAPTER TWELVE

"What are you so damn cheery about?" Mick asked. His mood was especially rank tonight. And he was clearly aggravated by Diana's new lease on life. "Last night you was in some sort of dream world," he complained. "Now, tonight, you're all perk. You on drugs or something?"

"What would be the point?" Diana teased. "Working for you is trippy enough."

"Smart mouth! I'm impressed. Is that what you do with your time off—you practice your one-liners?"

"Ba-dum-bum!" Diana sang, beating her imaginary drumsticks in the air, like an eager-to-please comedian giving the audience its cue to laugh. With a satisfied smile, she strutted away, leaving a stunned Mick behind to wonder when she'd gotten so vocal. In all the time she'd worked there, Diana had never done anything more than smirk at his unrobed insults. And for the old Diana, even a smirk was bold. But from now on, this girl who still had a lot of life in her was not going to be taking any crap from a man who began his put-downs with the words "You was."

On her way into the kitchen to take her break, Diana eyed the dessert case, as usual. But this time she caught sight of her reflection lingering behind the heaping hunk of strawberry shortcake that generally screamed her name at this most favored time of night. The jumbo strawberry in the cake's center covered her mouth, making her look like one of those dead dinner pigs she'd only seen in cartoons—the kind that laid on huge rectangular tables filled with food, flat on their bellies and dead as doornails, with giant apples stuffed in their mouths. The resemblance was so striking, and the comparison so vivid, that the whole concept of break cake lost its appeal entirely. Diana didn't want to be a dead pig.

Since she wasn't eating on her break, she decided to make a list of everything she wanted to do with her new life. She called it Diana's "My Life is Far From Over" List, and it read:

1. *Be skinny.*
2. *Find happier job.*
3. *Have sex again before I die.*

It's 6:00 a.m., and I'm Lauren Prescott, happy to be joining you on what the weather guys here at 102.1 W-ERD tell me is going to be a beautiful *day. This next song should help get yours started quite nicely.*

Diana struggled to keep the lid on her excitement during the music's first few notes of play, for one of her biggest pet peeves with radio was getting all excited at the start of a song she thought she loved, only to realize a few seconds into it that it was a completely different song than the one she was thinking of, which always made her resent the impostor song, as well as herself for being such a musical idiot. So, in order to reduce her chances of disappointment and embarrassment over something as annoyingly trivial as a song on the car radio, she had learned to just wait for the lyrics.

Well, you're the real tough cookie with the long history… And there they were. Breathing a sigh of relief, Diana knew she could get excited now, for this was unmistakably Pat Benatar. Throbbing with an adrenaline that made her feel more vibrant than the ascending sun, she turned up the volume, way past its usual one o'clock position, to let God and the angels know she was ready to live life in full blast. Moderation, always being a sideline spectator, hadn't gotten her very far. She wanted to scream "Hit Me with Your Best Shot" to the world. So that's exactly what she did—driving 43 mph in a 35 mph zone the whole way home, and passing The Doughnut Bin without even pausing to be proud that she hadn't stopped. She was too busy singing to notice. Next time, she'd start enjoying the song as soon as she had the impulse. And if it turned out to be an impostor, well she'd just roll down her window and laugh like a hyena to show the whole damn town that she'd never witnessed anything as funny as herself. After all, the ability to laugh at oneself was rumored in her women's magazines to be a highly attractive quality—one that, if mastered, could probably help her achieve number three on her list of goals a little sooner than just before the end of time.

CHAPTER THIRTEEN

June 5th

Dear Diary (or Old Notebook That I'm Using as a Diary Because I Did Not Feel Like Buying One),

I've decided it would be a good idea to keep track of my weight loss—and all of my men—in here. So far I haven't lost any weight and I haven't met any men. But that's because today is the first day of the rest of my life. Well, actually, yesterday afternoon was. But this is the first full day. I owe it all to Mrs. Bartle and something she said while we were having tea. It turns out that we're both full of life. I don't know—I can't really explain it all. What I do know, however, is that I am five-foot-four-and-a-half inches tall and I weigh 178 pounds, and the last time I slept with a man was when I was still a girl. I want to weigh 130 pounds. And I want to find love.

But if not, I'd settle for 140 pounds and a lot of sex, preferably in a bed.
Diana

CHAPTER FOURTEEN

The hot pellets of water bounced from Diana's face and shoulders, slithering down the numerous curves of her body to the warm sudsy pool on the shower floor. Had showers always felt this good? Diana could not remember the last time a shower had been anything more than going through the motions of proper hygiene. *Life* had been about nothing more than going through the motions of existence. But that was all changed now. As she reached for the shampoo, her eyes were drawn to the cubic zirconia stone on her left hand. Her mother was right—it did look like an engagement ring. Not that it wasn't lovely, but how would she woo the men if they all thought she was engaged? Diana made a mental note: *Return ring.* And then, as the warm water continued to glide over her body like an endless stream of healing aphrodisiac, her thoughts returned to the sensual and soothing powers of the almighty shower, and she couldn't help but feel lust. But it was more than sexual lust. It was a lust for experience, for living with bright eyes fixated on a future that included more than self-loathing and strawberry shortcake. This was the first shower she'd taken since her rebirth in the living room with Mrs. Bartle. She would let it be her baptism: washing away all prenatal sin, most especially the sin of hating herself for twenty-six years, she would emerge from the bathroom with a spirit cleansed for a life renewed. She felt thinner already.

Diana got out of the shower, and as she stood there towel-drying the beads of holy water that still clung to her baby-fresh skin, she heard her mother's voice blaring from the answering machine, desperately trying to slither its way underneath the bathroom door. Mrs. Christopher was explaining, rather frantically, that she'd thought it over and that after the cancer scare and everything, she'd realized that nothing was more important than mother-daughter bonding, so even though she was tired from her new aerobic schedule, she was still willing to make the time for their weekly routine and really hoped that Diana had not made other plans, like with that sweet old lady *what's-her-name* from upstairs (*or was it down?*), but if she had, was there any way she could cancel them? In other words, she wanted to know if Diana could meet her at Ping's at 12:30.

On her way to the restaurant, Diana stopped at the post office to mail the controversial "engagement" ring back to EasyShop. It hadn't even been two weeks since she'd received it, and the host on the air had promised a thirty-day money-back guarantee. Before pulling out of the parking lot, Diana made a promise of her own and wrote it in her diary, which she'd decided to keep in her glove compartment whenever she left home so that she'd never really be without it. After all, it was important to record every success, every goal, every wish, and all occurrences worthy of entry as soon as they happened. In this case, she'd been struck with an excellent motivation for weight loss—a promise to save the $36.95 refund from the ring for a pair of size-ten jeans. And as a PS to that promise, Diana vowed not to buy them until she really *was* a size ten.

Now a size sixteen, she could still vividly remember the high school horror of being a twelve and stuffing herself into a ten every morning: the sigh of relief she'd breathe after completing the first hurdle, which was actually getting the pants over what she then viewed as her abnormally gigantic rear end (although now she'd thank her lucky stars for a size-twelve ass), before flopping backward onto her bed to fight with the zipper, which generally got stuck midway and had to either be cursed at *(Fucking piece of crap zipper!)*, coaxed along with baby talk *(Come on, we're almost there… There you go… Atta zipper!)*, or begged *(PLEASE don't do this to me! I'm going to be late for homeroom!)*. And then it would be off to school for a day of physical anguish with the denim inseams of her jeans chafing her thighs when she walked, and the waistband clawing at her stomach whenever she sat down.

She could still recall the wonderfully liberating feeling

of coming home to peel that torture-cast off of her body each afternoon. But looking back, the reward—that is, the luxurious appreciation of being able to breathe at the end of the day—was not rewarding *enough* for Diana to even consider partaking of that lifestyle again. Sure, sometimes her size sixteens got a little tight in the stomach after a large meal, which is why she often unbuttoned them under the table when she went out to eat. But for the most part, she knew she was a true size sixteen. And these painful memories of her size-twelve-denial days made her realize that she'd rather stay a true sixteen than be a mock ten that spent at least half of her waking hours trying to learn how to breathe without busting out of her clothes. But something told Diana that in time she'd be able to fit all of her life-lusting vitality into a size ten *without* wishing an attached respirator were the "must have" accessory piece of the season. And that vision alone was more to live for than any azalea-adorned tumor blimp in the clouds.

CHAPTER FIFTEEN

"How's your mother, dear?"

Mrs. Bartle's question was the same every Thursday. And Diana always appreciated it. Rather than asking how lunch was—because she knew the answer would be negative—Mrs. Bartle simply asked how her mom was, leaving the decision to complain or merely say "fine" solely up to Diana. And usually, unless she really needed to vent, "fine" was just about all Diana ever said. But today was very different. Today, Diana said "good." And Mrs. Bartle almost dropped her teacup.

"Good?" she asked, smiling as she braced herself for a story.

"Good," Diana said matter-of-factly, sipping her tea in an ever-so-nonchalant fashion, and just waiting for her completely unintrusive friend who had innocently taken the bait to swallow it and beg for more. And that's exactly what Mrs. Bartle did.

"Good as in good?" she pressed eagerly. Diana smiled. She knew it had to be the first time in this woman's entire life that she'd ever attempted to pry. She wasn't very good at it.

"Good as in good," Diana echoed, teasing her a little. But seeing that Mrs. Bartle was about to give up, she threw her another line. "Well, good as in I had an enjoyable time."

"An enjoyable time?"

"Yes."

"Enjoyable as in fun?"

"Enjoyable as in fun."

"Fun, huh?"

"Fun, yes."

"Good." And a discouraged Mrs. Bartle turned back to her tea. Diana could see this was going to take a while.

What she did eventually end up telling Mrs. Bartle was that she and her mother had laughed that afternoon. Like really and truly *laughed*. It hadn't been over anything especially poignant or symbolic, just Mrs. Christopher's inability to understand the waiter's Chinese accent when he'd asked if she wanted a fork to replace the one she'd dropped on the floor. Judging by her mother's startled expression and the blushing manner in which she shook her head *no thank you,* Diana knew that her ears had heard something different, and she had to explain to Mrs. Christopher that "Wanna fuck?" was probably not the offer he'd made. The relief on her mother's face had caused Diana to smile, which, in turn, made her mother laugh. It was a genuine laugh, freakishly yet comfortingly unlike the usual *ha-ha*'s that every so often emerged from this woman whose sense of humor tended to take incredibly long vacations. The queen of condescending *You-had-to-be-there*'s and *I'm-laughing-AT-you-and-not-with-you*'s had actually broken into an honest and uncontrollable bout of giggles. And it was one that was intriguingly contagious, for pretty soon their table shook with a rumbling, two-sided laughter that made Diana drop her own *fuck* on the floor. The waiter then rushed over to offer another *fuck,* propelling the eye-tearing laugh fest into serious overtime. Of course, Diana didn't tell Mrs. Bartle these details. No matter how close the two of them were, she just couldn't bring herself to mention the f-word in front of her. But it didn't matter anyway because Mrs. Bartle wouldn't be asking what had been so funny—she'd already reached her life's prying limit by getting Diana to disclose the fact that she and her mother had laughed; over what wasn't really important. What *was* important was that Diana had gotten through a lunch with her mother without wanting to kill anybody—not even herself.

On the way to their cars, Diana had felt an incredible urge to tell her mother all about her new weight loss incentive. She'd wanted to say, *Hey Mom, guess what? I didn't eat anything fattening on my break. And I skipped my chocolate banana muffin and large coffee with hazelnut cream this morning.* But then her secret would have been out, and Mrs. Christopher would have known that Diana had gotten fat by actually *eating* fattening food. There'd be no more playing of the innocent *I-don't-know-why-I-keep-gaining-weight* card, which was the one she always carried around her mother in order to avoid being branded with the added stigmas of being gluttonous, unmotivated and out-of-control, in addition to fat—these other things were easier to hide, and Mrs. Christopher need not know about them. The truth was that Diana knew perfectly well that strawberry shortcake and muffins from The Dough-nut Bin were fattening, but she'd always figured that since God had already denied her all other pleasures in life, she might as well indulge herself in the ones that were at her fingertips, even if the gratification she got from them was fleeting. Up until yesterday, that had been her rationale, a rationale she was not about to even consider trying to explain to her mother now that she'd discarded it. So she didn't tell her about that day's dieting triumphs. And keeping her weight loss goal undercover made her feel like she had something important going on, something private, something that even her know-it-all mother didn't know about. For the first time since Barry and the pickup truck, she felt like she had a life.

CHAPTER SIXTEEN

Saturday night at Scott's Tavern. Supposedly *the* happening time and place for singles—at least according to the two women behind Diana in line at the dry cleaners that morning, the ones whose conversation she could not help but overhear. It had gone something like:

So, do you think Billy will be at Scott's tonight?

(Gasp) I thought you were SO over him!

I am. But that doesn't mean I shouldn't try to look hot in case he shows up.

Point taken… What time are we heading over?

Probably around ten—fuck, I hope Pat doesn't show up.

Pat?

Shit! I mean Pete! (giggle)

Do I need to buy you one of those little black books now so you can keep track of all your—

Shut up, it's not like I'm a slut. If it weren't for Scott's Tavern, I'd practically be a virgin. I can't help that there's so many hot single guys there.

Or so many hot guys that want you to THINK they're single.

Well, them either.

Or the ones who only look hot after your fifth beer.

Okay, them either. But what I'm saying is that the men I bring home from Scott's—and it's ONLY been nine in an EN-TIRE year—anyway, they don't count. I mean they count, but not as much as if I'd found them at some random variety of other clubs or bars. At least I pick them all up in one place.

You pick THEM up? I thought they picked YOU up.

Fuck you.

No thanks.

Seated at the bar now, Diana played the conversation over again in her mind. Nine sex partners in a year sure seemed like a lot to her. But then again, what did she know? Not a lot, probably. At least not yet. That was why she was here, at Scott's Tavern—to learn. Of course, she was somewhat uncomfortable being here by herself, but she knew that in order to meet men, she had to venture out of her apartment building, even if she had no friends to venture with. This wasn't exactly the kind of place she could bring Mrs. Bartle to. But Diana was armed with a brand-new sense of confidence. Or at least this was what she thought confidence must feel like, but she couldn't be totally positive because she'd never really had any.

Dressed in the carnation-pink blouse and black,

pleated, knee-length skirt she'd worn to her mother's house on Easter, with her strawberry-blond hair dancing in loose, silky ringlets to her shoulders, Diana felt pretty for the first time in a long time. The look had been surprisingly effortless to achieve, considering that this was the only nice outfit she had to choose from and that her hair, which was so accustomed to being pulled up into a sloppy, half-assed bun for work, was naturally curly to begin with, a fact she'd forgotten could be an asset. She'd even bought a deliciously sweet, yet subtle bottle of perfume at the drugstore. It was called "Siren" and was designed to emulate the fragrances worn by the great screen sirens of Hollywood yesteryear. Diana had never been close enough to Greta Garbo, Rita Hayworth or Jean Harlow to know what they smelled like, but she imagined it couldn't have been much sexier than this. Diana couldn't even *remember* the last time she had worn perfume. She remembered the last time she wore cologne, though—New Year's 1988, after Barry had rubbed his scent all over her body in the back of his legendary powder blue pickup truck. And even though they had done the "dirty deed," Diana didn't shower for two days afterward—not because she'd wanted to feel close to him or anything corny like that, but because she'd wanted to feel naughty for as long as she could, and the smell of Barry reminded her of just how naughty she had been. It was 11:03 p.m. She'd been at this singles' haven since a quarter to ten, and had slowly nursed two root beers waiting for some kind of action to start. Perhaps it was time for a real drink. Maybe some alcohol would up the number of guys she'd been confident enough to speak to since she'd arrived. So far, she had spoken to one: the college-age bartender who had served her the sodas, the one who'd looked at her strangely when she'd asked if he needed to see her ID, and even more strangely when she'd joked, "Or maybe I should ask to see *yours.*" Apparently, Sense of Humor was not this guy's middle name. She didn't even need his ID to figure that one out.

"Another root beer?"

"No, I think I'll take a regular beer."

"All right, what'll it be?"

"Surprise me," Diana said. She knew nothing about beer. The last time she'd had any was at her mother's company picnic three years ago, but it had tasted so bad—like chilled urine with foam—that she'd pretended to spill hers, then got lectured the entire way home for acting drunk in front of Mrs. Christopher's colleagues. Fortunately, this beer didn't taste as bad as she remembered it. It wasn't as good as soda or chocolate milk, and it was definitely not something she'd drink if it wasn't rumored to diminish one's inhibitions—for when it came to approaching men, Diana's inhibitions needed all the diminishing they could get—but at least it was ingestible. And sipping it made her feel more at ease. But it wasn't until midway through her second beer that Diana began to understand the altered state of consciousness commonly referred to as "buzzed" by people who had social lives. Like Brooke from the diner, who was always bragging to someone on the phone during her breaks about how "totally buzzed" she was at so-and-so's party. Diana's head felt light. In fact, her entire body felt light, which, through this brilliantly pleasant and unfamiliar haze, made her feel like laughing. She felt happy, giddy even. Could this be why people drank? Another one of these and she'd be able to talk to anyone. Even the cutest guy in the bar. *Even* the one with the blond hair shooting pool by the ladies' room, who was quite possibly the most attractive man alive.

Leaning back in her seat to let her new best friend, the Buzz, wash over her, Diana began thinking of all the things she needed to buy before she could be a truly sexy woman. Lipstick was key. Since arriving at the bar, she had not seen one woman with nude lips. Diana had never really gotten into makeup, always wondering what the point would be—it couldn't change her; cosmetics would only turn her into a *decorated* fat person. But that was the old Diana. The new Diana realized that the road to her thin and sexy self should definitely include lipstick, and that even if she were to be stuck in the Heavyweight/Celibate-for-Fifteen-Years *(but-not-by-choice)* Division for months, she'd be better off with moist, pouty and seductive lips to see her through. And she wouldn't make her move on that blond, pool-playing god by the ladies' room until after she'd attained the proper lips. For as the saying went, *A smile is worth a thousand words.* Or was it, *A picture is worth a thousand smiles?*

While Diana's mind tingled with confusion at the

challenge of deciphering old adages to make them pertain to lipstick, one thing became unmistakably clear: this feeling—the one she had right now—*this* was why people drank.

CHAPTER SEVENTEEN

If Diana's first real singles nightlife experience had proven anything, besides the necessity of lipstick, it was that she needed to update her wardrobe. The only nice clothes she owned were the ones she'd debuted in at Scott's Tavern last week. She couldn't exactly get away with wearing her Easter outfit *every* Saturday night. That outfit was a little conservative for the bar scene anyway. What Diana needed were some downright sexy clothes. And if she could find them in her size, she was going to wear them.

It used to be a mortifying thought—a large woman at-tempting sex appeal in a size-sixteen version of something that should never have been manufactured past a ten. But Diana's new lease on life included a new clause on her relationship to the fashion industry: if it's sexy, and they make it, and it fits, it will be bought. Diana knew it could take months until she was the size she'd always wanted to be, but why waste those months hiding out in potato sacks? Did overweight women not deserve to feel sexy? Because Diana had not only been feeling sexy since she'd ventured out of her cocoon—she'd been feeling *damned* sexy. Memories of Barry had begun to heat her bed each night, and she knew it would only be a matter of time before those memories were replaced by the real thing. Well, not exactly the *real* thing. It wasn't like she was on some sort of psychotic quest to find the long-lost love of her life or anything. Besides, what would she want with the real Barry anyway? He had to be forty-three by now and was probably balding. No, for Diana the "real thing" simply meant a warm body of the opposite sex that could replace her fifteen-year-old memories with action—and hopefully a lot of it—in the here and now. The desire, and the confidence that it would be fulfilled, made her feel like a smoking circuit of sexual energy. Lust coursed wildly through her veins, casting a radiant glow that shined through her eyes and skin. She felt dazzling and dangerous, like a predator—and not one who stalked strawberry shortcake and fatty breakfast muffins, but one who stalked life and sex. And the idea that how people are perceived by others is contingent upon the way they perceive themselves gave her hope—hope that every man who saw her, saw her as an undeniably hot force that he could only dream of reckoning with. Now all she needed was a new outfit to match her new image.

It had to be an outfit that gave her *in-your-face* confidence, far less subtle than the silent celebration of sexiness she'd been carting around in her strut. Not that she wasn't off to a great start by acknowledging her inner goddess, but now she wanted the fact that she was desirable and confident to be unmistakably obvious to more than just herself. She needed verbal confidence now, the kind that would lift her over the threshold of bystander and make her a player. She wanted to be able to go up to that blond, pool-playing miracle of nature she'd seen at Scott's and *make* him notice her—by engaging him in a real, live conversation, as opposed to just a series of longing, one-sided stares from across the bar. But first she needed the proper equipment.

She'd already taken care of the lipstick void, but that honestly hadn't been too much fun. The teenage clerk at Taylor's Pharmacy in the mall had gawked at Diana like she was a circus freak when she'd asked what color the girl would recommend for her lips.

"Uh, I don't know," the clerk had finally stammered. "Pink?"

"Well, what shade of pink would you suggest?" Diana had asked enthusiastically, while the girl stared at her in a horrified, yet hauntingly familiar way. It was the way Diana used to look at her mother when she was a teenager and Mrs. Christopher was severely embarrassing her in public, the way she'd looked at her just last week in Dr. Mason's office when she'd suggested that Diana had willed herself into a false pregnancy.

"Well, uh…" the clerk had begun. A line of customers had formed behind Diana, and some of them looked very annoyed. "Makeup's in aisle four… Can I help you?"

she'd asked, looking over Diana's shoulder to the next in line.

A little hurt, and not exactly sure what she had done to incur such rudeness, Diana had left the line and found her way to cosmetics, where, in order to make sure she didn't miss anything, she'd spent over half an hour picking up each and every tube of lipstick and reading the color names aloud to keep them straight in her mind. Occasionally, she just had to stop and laugh. Some of their names were just plain ridiculous! "Vanilla Brownie," "Sunset" and "Poison Ivy" were *colors?*

She had finally settled on "Malibu Pink"—at least there was a color in the name—when the clerk she'd consulted with earlier began leading a mall security guard down the aisle. They seemed to be headed right in her direction. Diana feared they thought she was shoplifting, so to put an end to their suspicions, she'd exclaimed, with what in retrospect seemed like perhaps a little too much enthusiasm but at the time seemed applause-worthy clever, "I've found it! Malibu Pink!" Proudly waving her intended purchase before the guard's eyes, she had slipped by before he could make any accusations. And as she went, she tossed her hair haughtily in the direction of the clerk whose face bore a squeamish look of apology for wasting security's time. Diana had then paid for the lipstick and gotten the hell out of there. Who would've guessed that buying makeup could be so tremendously difficult?

★ ★ ★

"Can I help you to find anything today?" asked a big, jolly saleswoman with bright pink cheeks. Diana had just entered The Queen's Closet, a store whose sign boasted Fabulous fashions for *real*-sized women. Translation: *We specialize in fat clothes.*

"Yes. I'm looking for something, um…" Diana was suddenly embarrassed. How could she tell this cheery, wholesome, mother-of-three-ish type that she was looking for slut clothes?

"Dressy?" the woman offered.

"Sort of. I'm actually looking for, you know, um…*singles* clothes," Diana said, winking at the saleslady in a *We-both-know-what-I-REALLY-mean* sort of way, and inwardly marveling at her own tactfulness. Unfortunately, good old Pink Cheeks didn't understand and therefore couldn't appreciate Diana's talent for tact, proving that she had absolutely no concept of sisterhood, no from-one-heavy-girl-to-another sensibilities. For the sales clerk took "singles" to mean separates, and told Diana that at The Queen's Closet everything was mix-and-match because they understood that "real" women weren't always the same size on top as they were on the bottom. Seeing that this woman was going to be no help at all, Diana pretended to be relieved at the store's innovative and humane sizing policies, and said she'd just look around for a little while, which seemed to please old Pink Cheeks.

In the dressing room, Diana noticed something startling. She couldn't be positive but it seemed her right thigh had gotten smaller. Right then and there, she vowed

not to return home without a bathroom scale. Meanwhile, she'd also found an outfit: fitted, black, satin pants
and a shimmery, short-sleeved, silver top with black trim
around the arms and neckline. It cost $112—about seven
weeks' worth of chocolate banana muffins and large
hazelnut cream coffees. But she'd already made her down
payment this week—she hadn't gone to The Doughnut
Bin once. Six more weeks of good behavior and the outfit would pay for itself. Of course, at the rate her right
thigh appeared to be going, in six weeks she might not
be able to wear it. However, not fitting into clothes because they were too *big* would be a problem Diana could
get used to.

CHAPTER EIGHTEEN

June 14th

Dear Diary,

I lost six pounds! Actually, it could be more than six because the last time I got weighed on a regular scale was at Mom's house over two months ago, and it said 178, but there's always a chance that I gained weight since then, before getting down to…172!—which is what I weighed on my new scale just now. But then again, if her scale is a few pounds ahead of mine (like those damned doctor's office scales that always say you weigh more than you do on any other scale on the planet, and which I personally refuse to go by), and I hadn't gained any weight since then, then I may have actually lost less than six pounds. But in any case, my right thigh is noticeably smaller than it was last week, so I know I had to have lost some weight. But on to the next subject: blond, pool-playing god-man from

Scott's Tavern. There are no excuses for me not to talk to him tonight, for I now have lipstick and a sexy outfit to wear. Hopefully next time I write, I'll have something even more exciting to report on than the incredible shrinking right thigh.
Diana

PS—But if I don't, I'll be more than happy to settle for an update on the progress of the left one.

CHAPTER NINETEEN

"You look *incredible,* dear!" Mrs. Bartle was just about to knock on Diana's door when she opened it to leave.

"Oh, Mrs. Bartle, you scared me! I was just about to leave."

"I can see that. It looks like you've sure got someplace to be!"

Diana knew that in all the time Mrs. Bartle had known her, she'd never seen her sparkle like this. In fact, she'd never seen her sparkle at all. Unfortunately, Diana didn't know how to tell her ninety-three-year-old friend that she was going out to try her luck at picking up a man she'd seen playing pool at a bar so that she could bring him home and have sex with him and then write about it in her diary. But thankfully, Mrs. Bartle wasn't the nosy type, and Diana knew she wouldn't even ask where this "someplace" was, let alone what she was planning to do once she got there. She could always count on good old Mrs. Bartle not to put her in an awkward situation.

"Where are you going?" Or maybe she couldn't. Apparently, that bit of prying practice the other day regarding Diana's lunch with her mother had emboldened the once angelically unintrusive Mrs. Bartle.

"I'm just going out for a drink."

"Oh, that sounds like fun, dear."

"Yeah, well, I figure it's a Saturday night, you know, something to do." Why was she making excuses? It wasn't as if she were doing anything illegal. But somehow she felt like a teenager in a TV show who was lying to her parents about going to the library when she was really sneaking off to some wild, out-of-her-league party that home audiences already knew from the previews would be busted by the cops. "Why don't you come in?"

"Oh, no, that's all right, dear. Ruthie Silverman is coming for dinner. We rented *Where the Boys Are,* and I was going to ask you to join us. But that was before I saw you. Now, as your friend and elder, I will not permit you to waste that outfit and that hair on an evening watching television with two old ladies. You get out there and have a good time. Here, let me walk you downstairs."

Diana smiled gratefully, closing the door behind them. When they reached Mrs. Bartle's door, she wanted to throw her arms around her friend and rave about how hot this guy from Scott's was. She wanted to ask her what she thought of the new Diana. She wanted to tell her how their friendship had saved her life. But all she said was, "Have a great time with Mrs. Silverman tonight."

"You have a great time, too," Mrs. Bartle said, twitching her nose a little as she leaned closer to Diana. "You smell delicious! What perfume is that?"

"It's called Siren," Diana said proudly. "Supposedly, it smells like the fragrances that Hollywood's great screen sirens used to wear. You know, like in the thirties."

"Well, that's lovely," Mrs. Bartle said. "Did you know that in Greek mythology, a siren was one of a group of sea nymphs whose voices were so intoxicatingly sweet, they lured sailors to destruction just by singing their songs?" Diana shook her head, impressed. Mrs. Bartle seemed to know so many things, and she always found such a timely way of sharing what she knew. "Anyway," her friend continued, "you have a great time tonight. You *deserve* it."

"Thanks, Mrs. Bartle," Diana said. But she hoped her eyes said a lot more. As the two women stood there, looking at one another with an almost psychic kind of understanding, Diana knew that Mrs. Bartle had an idea of what she was up to. And she wanted her to know that she couldn't be more thankful for her blessing. There was a tremendous sense of comfort—and, admittedly at times, a little eeriness—in the way this woman knew her. It was an amazing relief to realize that someone cared enough about her to *really* know her, someone that paid attention to her inner struggles and aspirations in a way her own mother never had.

"And don't go singing to any drunken sailors while

you're out, my little siren," Mrs. Bartle teased as her slight form disappeared behind door 101 A.

Diana stood there for a few seconds thinking about how lucky she was to have such a wealth of wisdom and understanding in her life—all bundled up into one tiny package that had proven itself on countless occasions to be her very best friend. She had just turned to go when the voice of the bundle bellowed out, desperate and concerned, from behind the closed door.

"Diana?"

"Yeah, Mrs. Bartle? Are you all right? Did you need me?"

"No, I…" The muffled little voice on the other side of the door faltered beneath the excited, Saturday-night rantings of the fresh-faced twenty-somethings that had just entered the building, each of them armed with at least one six-pack of beer.

"Mrs. Bartle, I can't hear you. Should I come in?"

"I said…" Her voice was audible now, probably because the twenty-somethings had caught a glimpse of their elder, namely Diana, standing by the stairwell, and out of what was likely an attempt at respect, had reduced their brash enthusiasm to a refined racket. "…these are dangerous times," Mrs. Bartle continued as the racket grew even softer. "So make sure your gentleman friend wears a rubber. And if he says, 'I forgot it,' you tell him to *forget* it. It's as simple as that."

Diana could feel a dozen pairs of twenty-something eyes peering into her from every angle, but for what was probably the first time ever, she really didn't care what other people thought. "Other people" weren't as lucky as she was anyway. These kids didn't *have* a Mrs. Bartle in their lives. Door 101 A didn't filter precious pearls of advice for *them*.

"It's like my mother used to tell me," the voice behind the door continued, "if you're going to let snakes roam around in your garden, at least be sure they're wearing their raincoats… And, Diana?"

"Yes," Diana said. "I'm still listening."

"If he gives you any trouble, you tell him to come see me."

CHAPTER TWENTY

After Diana's father died, her mother became an ice queen who immersed herself in interior design and eventually made it a career. In less than two years, Mrs. Christopher had joined one of the city's most prestigious decorating firms, which left little time for her to enjoy the home she'd so zealously recreated in her efforts to purge the place of sad memories. And so Diana was left alone a lot of the time, with no mother and no father, in a house where nothing was comforting or familiar or in any way like it used to be. When Mrs. Christopher *was* around, she was always busy trying to make up for her many absences, which she did through "connecting" with her daughter—or, in other words, criticizing every move Diana made in order to demonstrate her "heartfelt" concern and ability to parent effectively in spite of her time constraints. When Diana was eight, nine and ten, it was her handwriting, her dirty fingernails and her mathematical ineptitude that served as the basis for their bond. And then, once she got older and started—and never quite stopped—filling out, it was all about her weight.

At first it was, "Why don't we see if the doctor can give us the number of a good children's obesity specialist?" And then it was refusing to let Diana have ice cream when she had her tonsils removed. Even though it was all they ate in the movies and on television after such a procedure, ice cream was forbidden in the Christopher house, and was replaced by apricot and skim milk smoothies. Although this seemed like a cruel way to treat a patient, her mother continued to remind her that her thighs would be grateful later and that Diana had already weaseled one bowl of the stuff out of that damned hospital staff that had disobeyed her explicit orders to the contrary. And then it was buying a giant padlock for the refrigerator doors and refusing to give Diana the combination when she'd come home from school starving for a snack. "Go for a walk," Mrs. Christopher would say when Diana would call her at work, begging. So that's exactly what Diana would do—she'd walk right down the road to Suzy Newman's house and, together, they'd eat until they were stuffed. Then they'd lie on their backs on the living room floor and watch "Wheel of Fortune" on Suzy's big screen TV. Suzy was skinny and her parents were rich. They owned Yosie's Gourmet Deli on the corner of Ivywood and Blaine, two of the poshest streets in the wealthiest section of town. They didn't care if Suzy overate, and it didn't matter one bit to them if her poor, fatherless, fat friend down the road devoured half of their food. Diana had loved the Newmans. But they moved when she was fourteen, and she and Suzy had lost touch after that. They'd tried to stay friendly through letters, but without bingeing and Pat Sajak to keep them close every afternoon, the friendship began to seem artificial. But fortunately for Diana, Suzy's move did not deliver her back to a life of after-school hunger; for Mrs. Christopher, seeing that her brilliant locking-the-refrigerator idea had done absolutely nothing to take her daughter's weight off, had opened the doors of afternoon snacking to Diana months before the Newmans left town. But that was all adolescence.

The real fun didn't start until Diana was sixteen and no one asked her to the junior prom. From then on out, her mother tried the gentle, nagging, *I'll-remind-you-every-chance-I-get-how-completely-fat-and-inadequate-you-are-but-it's-really-for-your-own-good-and-not-because-I-enjoy-putting-you-down (it's-just-that-you-keep-giving-me-reason-to)* approach. "Diana, isn't that your third slice of pizza?" she would ask. "You know, now would be a good time to start losing weight for *next* year's prom. That's the one that really counts," she would say. "Oh, honey, imagine if you don't get asked to your senior prom. You'll regret it for the rest of your life!"

And when Diana wasn't asked: "Let's go out to dinner, Diana—you and me. It'll take your mind off of the prom. Besides, I've got a surprise for you: it's a special diet that allows you to lose weight while still dining at all of your favorite restaurants. I ordered it weeks ago to cheer you up when—I mean, in case—you weren't asked to the prom."

And when the diet didn't work: "Diana, just because you're allowed to eat all of your favorite foods, it doesn't mean you're supposed to eat them all in one sitting! You know, we really haven't had much success with any method I've tried, but that's because *you* have to try, too! I think it's time for an intervention, for I just simply don't know what to do with you anymore. Let's see what Dr. Mason has to say."

And when Dr. Mason gave medical confirmation to the layman's diagnosis that Diana was, indeed, overweight, it was: "Uh-uh-uh, Diana! Remember Dr. Mason's orders—no junk food. Why not have a protein shake? That way you can skip dinner, and just be done eating for the day." And then her mother would smile like she was doing a commercial for the stuff, probably figuring her enthusiasm could brainwash Diana into thinking the meal replacement powder was a treat instead of a punishment.

But nothing was worse than those terrible looks of pity that started after the big 28 hit. That was when Mrs. Christopher was struck especially hard with the reality that Diana had been living outside of the cruel social caste system of high school for ten years and *still* had no boyfriend. Worse yet, she was still fat—fatter even. And since she had moved out and gotten her own place a couple years earlier, Mrs. Christopher could no longer even attempt to control what went into her daughter's mouth. Except when they were at

Ping's—but that was only one measly meal out of an entire week's worth of fat, calories, carbs and bad choices.

However, Diana supposed that the absolute creepiest thing about her relationship with her mother was the fact that they'd never discussed her father's death. And even more disturbing was the reason why. Ever since she was old enough to recognize fear in others, she had sensed that her mother harbored a suspicion that she'd give her life to make untrue. Diana knew that deep down her mother knew her secret. She knew that Diana had resented the ground she walked on the day Daddy left her with Mrs. Kingsly. "Let Mommy go to the seashore by herself." She knew what Diana had said. "One more story!" She knew how Diana had begged. *Maybe he'll be too tired to go. Maybe he won't leave. Maybe me and Daddy can have our OWN weekend, away from Mommy.* She knew what Diana had wished. Her mother knew about all of it—she knew that Diana had killed her father. And it seemed that Mrs. Christopher *thought* she knew something else—that in her daughter's eyes, the wrong parent had lived, that it should have been *her* in that explosion, and that if Diana could reverse God's order, she'd sacrifice her own mother to get her father back. But that was completely untrue. In fact, Diana was highly committed to the contrary—to preserving the life of the only parent she had left. And this meant not getting too close. For despite everything—every ounce of nagging and every obnoxious put-down—Diana loved her mother, and she didn't want to lose her.

★ ★ ★

"Can I get you another one?" The bartender's voice reeled her back into the reality of Saturday night single-hood at Scott's. Beer, sex and music—*that's* what Saturday nights were about, not morbid thoughts on one's mother and a past that couldn't be changed.

"You read my mind," Diana said. It was an outright lie, but it seemed to make the bartender smile. In truth, where her next drink was coming from was a suitable Saturday night concern, and one she would've already had if the good-natured, maternal sincerity of the "Put Raincoats on Your Snakes" lecture that Mrs. Bartle had inherited from her mother hadn't left Diana wondering about the relationship she shared with her own mother, a woman who'd managed to know her for thirty-two years without ever really *knowing* her at all. And then there was Mrs. Bartle, who had known her less than one-tenth of that time and could read her like a favorite book she'd practically memorized. But with a full beer in hand now, it was time to let go of these thoughts and concentrate on what really mattered. So where was he?

Diana had been there for over an hour and hoped that during her relapse into unhappy thoughts, that godly blond pool player from last week may have shown up. She surveyed the room, but there was no sign of him. Of course, there *were* other men that she could probably hit on, but why waste her energy microwaving frozen pizza when a fresh, hot and delicious one was on its way to her door? Whoops, food analogy. As a woman on the road to thinness, Diana wished not to have those anymore. She had to keep in mind that in her *new* life, nothing was a bowl of cherries, the whole enchilada, as easy as pie, a piece of cake or the icing on it. And men could not be compared to pizza.

She was just about to hit the ladies' room for a *What-if-he-shows-up-and-I-look-like-total-crap-because-I-got-ready-hours-ago?* emergency face and hair check when in walked Mr. Let's Get It On. And at that moment, all surrounding noise ceased to exist as Scott's Tavern became one with her left ventricle—the whole bar beating to the exaggerated, gong-like sound of her overexcited heart. Or maybe it was his heart—his sexy, *do-me,* perfect heart—commanding everything and everyone to follow its tune. For in this singular, most precious moment, theirs were the only two hearts in the world. Everyone else was just a robot, every*thing* else just some sort of government-orchestrated illusion. Reality was her and him. And her face had grown hot enough to heat the farthest planet from the sun. But Pluto would have to wait. Diana needed to have a look in the mirror and make her move before the inevitability of last call turned her into a pumpkin. The only problem was that the most important man that had ever lived was by the pool tables now, which meant—*deep breath, six pounds, shrinking thigh, don't panic*—he was also right by the ladies' room.

The walk over there was hellish. Diana felt like she had a hanger in her shirt and a broom up her butt, and she wished she could be more casual, more relaxed, more like…well…him. *New outfit, Malibu Pink, confident thoughts.* She couldn't look at him. All she could do was disappear, behind the comforting shield of the bath-room door.

Once inside and safely out of view, Diana gave her-self one hell of a pep talk, focusing entirely on posi-tives—why she was a sex goddess, why he'd be lucky to get her, why, no matter what happened, she should be proud of herself for trying and therefore having no re-grets about what could have been. She was careful to stay away from self-bashing conditionals: *If you don't do this, you'll never get a boyfriend, and you'll always be a disap-pointment to your mother. If you don't do this, God will spit on you. If you don't do this, you will never know what love is and would have been better off in that stupid blimp with those azaleas.*

As she neared the end of her emergency self-therapy session, the ladies' room door swung open, catching her completely off guard and causing her to jump back.

"Don't act so frightened, honey," said the intruder. "Doors open all the time." Diana couldn't tell if this woman was joking with her or insulting her, so she pro-duced her best *ha-ha-ha/fuck you* smile, and opened the door to destiny.

Mr. Wonderful was taking his shot. Diana knew noth-ing about pool, but when she heard the guys com-mending him afterward, she knew it was time to make her mark.

"Nice shot." Translation: *I want you so bad I can't breathe. You are the sexiest man I have ever had the honor of potentially humiliating myself for. You are the sun, you are the rain. You are the wind beneath my wings. My endless love, my silver spring, my first, my last, my everything. We are the world.* Why was it taking him so long to answer? Didn't he know that her entire concept of self was riding on what he said next?

"Yeah, thanks." Translation: *Yeah, thanks.*

Diana heard someone snicker. Were they laughing at her? She couldn't tell; they had all gone back to the game. No one was paying any attention to her at all. Maybe she *hadn't* made her mark. Maybe fat girls *couldn't* be sexy— not even with lipstick, the perfect outfit and a fully charged libido that, after a decade-and-a-half hiatus, had finally decided to wake up and chug the beer.

CHAPTER TWENTY-1

"Come on, ladies! You can do it! What's more important than a great ass?"

Diana felt like a big, fat blueberry in her navy terry-
cloth jogging suit. And this fitness instructor had to be
the most annoying woman she had ever seen. Well, besides her mother, of course, who sported overly shiny,
black spandex shorts and a leopard-print leotard, and had
just shot the most exaggerated look of enthusiasm Diana's
way, as if to convey the message—through this sweaty
mist of heart palpitations and anorexics killing themselves to burn fat they couldn't spare—that she savored
the dual benefit of mother-daughter bonding through
vigorous aerobic exercise. Please. Diana knew her mother
well enough to know that more than half of her bliss was
born out of the satisfaction of being right—about Diana's

weight, that is, and the necessity of bringing it down. It was a *You-finally-listened-to-your-mother-and-realized-you-were-a-fat-ass-and-now-you're-doing-something-about-it* kind of satisfaction, a gloating satisfaction that was, of course, rooted in the strict belief that Diana couldn't possibly arrive at positive decisions on her own, but rather that her life was all about resisting, and ultimately recognizing and rejoicing in, her mother's profound wisdom. But the fact was that Diana *had* made this choice on her own. Her failed barroom seduction plan, rather than depressing her, had been the exact motivation she'd needed to get off her ass and make things happen. She wasn't going to sit around and wait for those extra pounds to drop off by only watching her diet. She was going to *fight* them off, even if it meant sweating every step of the way. She wasn't going to sit around waiting for the rest of her life to fall into place before finding a better job either. That, too, was being taken care of. After only two days of searching the Help Wanted's, she'd already arranged to interview for an assistant counselor position at Happy Start Nursery Camp.

Diana loved children and always had. Not that she wanted any of her own yet. But she loved the idea of taking care of other people's. She couldn't believe she hadn't considered a career in child care sooner. If she played her cards right, Happy Start would provide her with more than just seasonal work since the ad said to inquire about September job openings at the school. Her interview was set for Thursday, so if things went well, she could be facing Mr. "Yeah, Thanks" on Saturday as a whole new woman—one with a new job *and* three workouts under her belt, which should naturally need to be tightened a notch or two. Of course, she could thank her mother for workout number three, for when Diana had asked to join in her aerobic efforts, Mrs. Christopher had decided to increase her own two-day-a-week schedule and had eagerly signed them both up for the Friday class. Diana knew she'd done it to accelerate her daughter's transition into the thin offspring she'd been waiting for so many years to be proud of, but the motivation for her mother's zeal didn't matter—as long as Diana got thinner faster.

"Ladies, we've got a newcomer in our midst!" The instructor, who affectionately referred to herself as "Kel," as if the "ly" part were a burden too formal and stuffy to bestow upon her students, who should always just think of her as "one of the girls," was beaming at Diana from across the room. *Please no, please no, please no,* Diana silently begged. "Say hello to Diana, everybody!" *Oh God, don't. Don't.*

"HI DIANA!" *Fuck.* The room echoed with the sound of her name. Could this *get* any more horrifying?

"Diana is Patty Christopher's daughter!" Apparently so. The resounding chorus of *ooh*'s and *ah*'s that followed sounded so rehearsed that Diana wondered if her mother had paid for it with her enrollment fee. No random aerobics class acquaintances could be *this* excited to meet her daughter. These women had to be actors.

"Stick with us, Diana," Kel said as she panted through her squat thrusts, "and we'll have you looking as good as your mother in no time!"

Never before had anyone desired the power of telekinesis as badly as Diana did at this very moment. She glared intently at Kel, resenting her for this ridiculous, pseudo-sexual humping exercise she was making them do, and hoping that by some miracle, her stare would be able to knock this malnourished blonde on steroids flat on her gluteally superior ass. She hated Kel. She hated people who introduced themselves with the nicknames they wanted others to call them by, people who forced a faux camaraderie with everyone they met in order to make others feel like their equals—as if the common folk would otherwise quake with intimidation, not knowing that such high and mighty figures were actually regular people just like them. Talk about flattering yourself! And speaking of flattering, was it supposed to be a compliment when someone told a thirty-two-year-old woman that with enough huffing, puffing and pain, she might look as good as her fifty-four-year-old mother one day? The fact that Mrs. Christopher had the body of a twenty-five-year-old, and that Diana would kiss the ground to look even half as good, didn't change the fact that a class full of 120-pounders would now be keeping an eye on Patty's plump daughter and charting her progress.

"All right, ladies! Time for your favorite part of the routine—abs!"

Diana watched her mother drop eagerly to the floor, and wondered how it was that these women seemed more excited about toning their already flat tummies than Diana had been about starting a whole new life.

"Mrs. Bartle, I got the job!" Diana had gotten the call less than a minute ago and had sped immediately downstairs to share the exciting news.

"You got the job! Oh, Diana, I'm so thrilled for you! Working with children is such a rewarding experience. Well, you'll see. When do you start?"

"Well, the camp starts a week from Monday. And if they like me, then I'll get three weeks off at the end of the summer and start back up again as a teacher's aid in September."

"If they *like* you?" Mrs. Bartle asked, looking confused. For like war, famine, flood, disease, and all the other catastrophic disasters that have plagued great minds across the nations for centuries, the idea of anyone not liking

Diana was just too incomprehensible and cruel for her to understand. "They're going to *love* you."

"Thanks, Mrs. Bartle." If only the rest of the world could see her the way this woman did. If only everyone thought Diana were as lovable and strong. If only there were another soul in the world as genuine and as whole-hearted as Mrs. Bartle—and that soul were male and around her age. If only self-esteem came in a bottle and thigh-friendly chocolate grew on trees.

"Have you given Mick your two weeks' notice yet?" Mrs. Bartle asked.

"No, I just found out, just now."

Mrs. Bartle looked deeply touched. "And you came right down here to tell me."

"Well, of course," Diana said, smiling. Who could possibly be a better partner in enthusiasm? Certainly not her mother. When Diana had told her that she was interviewing for an assistant counselor's position at a nursery school camp, she could actually *see* her mother biting her tongue. She knew that Mrs. Christopher had been just burning to criticize, but the fact that she'd struggled to contain her "advice" had made Diana feel powerful. It meant that her mother must have noticed the positive changes in her—the six pounds, the exercise class, the way that being the big blueberry in the back of the room didn't make her want to drop *out* of the exercise class. Perhaps noticing these things had made her mother decide that criticism was no longer appropriate. Maybe when someone shows signs of an expanding self-image—and a shrinking physical one—the critic feels threatened, like her counsel will be laughed off or, at best, disregarded. So, Mrs. Christopher hadn't said anything at all. She'd just raised her eyebrows and forced the corners of her mouth up into an exaggerated *How wonderful!* smile. But Diana knew that deep down, regardless of whether or not she would have chosen that job for herself, Mrs. Christopher was impressed by her daughter's sudden boldness—making a career change totally out of the blue and seeking a job that would be about so much more than the money. Still, she had said nothing. But not Mrs. Bartle. Judging by how enthusiastic her friend had been about the interview, she knew there'd be no better way to celebrate her success if she did get the job than by going straight downstairs to share the news with the one person who'd be happiest to hear it, the person whose happiness had no ulterior motives or clouding disapproval but existed solely because *Diana* was happy.

"I am so glad for you, dear," Mrs. Bartle said. "Why don't you come in and meet my great-nephew?"

"You mean William?" Diana asked. Mrs. Bartle nodded as a giant smile brought new light to her face. "What's he doing in Baltimore?"

This great-nephew was the grandson of Mrs. Bartle's late brother, Norman. While she and Henry had never been able to have children of their own, she'd remained exceptionally close to Norman's kids, caring for them as they grew as if she were their second mother. Their children were like grandchildren to her, and when William came along—last, but not least—they'd developed an immediate bond. Her youngest "grandson" was not only one of her best friends today, but also her ultimate pride and joy. She loved to tell the story of how he started out from nothing, the son of an auto mechanic in a little shop in Baltimore, where he'd learned the family trade and had followed in his father's footsteps, all before going to business school and opening his own chain of auto repair shops out west under the family name, also Mrs. Bartle's maiden name, of Carr. Diana had always wondered if the story's ending would seem as sweet if, instead of Carr's Auto Repair, her great-nephew had ended up with a chain of shops called Smith's or Johnson's Auto Repair. Probably not.

"He's looking to open some shops on the East coast. Now that his divorce is final, he's thinking of moving out here again to be closer to his parents and the cooking of his auntie Rose." Mrs. Bartle was beaming with pride. Diana could tell she was just bursting to introduce this legendary great-nephew of hers. How incredibly considerate it had been of her to wait for the excitement of Diana's job announcement to settle before moving on to any exciting announcements of her own. And this *was* a big deal. After hearing so much about him over the years, Diana couldn't wait to meet William. She wondered if he'd heard as much about her as she'd heard about him. She hoped not.

"Aunt Rose, who's there?" a voice questioned from inside. How sweet. Judging by how long they'd been in the hallway, her great-nephew probably thought Diana was some hard-selling door-to-door salesperson taking advantage of an old lady's kindness, and he was trying to rescue her.

"We're coming right in, dear," Mrs. Bartle reassured him. And taking Diana gently by the arm, she led her into the living room.

The man who rose from the couch didn't look *anything* like any self-motivated great-nephew Diana had ever envisioned—this man was hot! He was about five to ten years older than she was, with brown hair and that truly masculine sexiness that could only be described as "rugged good looks." But this was Mrs. Bartle's great-nephew, for Lord's sake. To entertain the thoughts she was starting to have was practically *incestuous.* Besides, Diana had already committed herself to Mr. Wonderful, aka "Yeah, Thanks."

"This," Mrs. Bartle said, beginning the introductions with her hand on Diana's shoulder, "is my very good friend from upstairs—"

"Diana?" the handsome stranger asked, staring at his great-aunt's visitor as if he'd known her in another life.

"Well, yes!" Mrs. Bartle laughed. She turned to Diana. "As you can see, I brag about *both* of my kids equally. And now you finally get to meet!" Diana smiled warmly, loving that she'd been referred to as one of Mrs. Bartle's "kids." But she didn't think this William guy was just putting two and two together. He seemed to know something. And his stare had grown hauntingly familiar. "*This,*" Mrs. Bartle announced proudly, joining him at his side to polish off the introductions, "is my famous great-nephew, William Barron Carr, but he'll probably prefer if you just call him—"

"Barry?"

Diana couldn't move, breathe or blink. And apparently neither could he. And so they just stood there—united by a one-night stand, separated for fifteen years, and brought together again by one incredible old lady who meant the world to both of them—frozen. For Diana, life had just drained itself of all credibility. Reality had taken a major nosedive, and she didn't know how she'd ever believe anything it dealt her ever again. Things like this didn't *really* happen. Or did they? Maybe Fate had a different sense of humor than that straight-laced barrel of ordinary they called Reality. One thing was certain: out of all the men in the world that Diana had ever slept with—which was one—she'd managed to make him the great-nephew of the only true friend she'd ever had.

"You two…have met before?" Poor Mrs. Bartle looked back and forth at the faces of her two favorite young people, struggling to make sense of the paralyzed thrill that hung in the air between them.

Diana nodded clumsily, her eyes still fixed upon Barry. She wanted to think poorly of him. After all, she'd certainly seen enough movies and talk shows since she was seventeen to know that Barry hadn't treated her very well after they did it. The guy wasn't supposed to hand you a wad of tissues and take off, leaving you cold and alone in the freezing and unfamiliar 1988 air. He was supposed to kiss you goodbye and ask for your number—even if he never planned to use it. But for some reason, she just couldn't dismiss him as a jerk. Perhaps it was because of his bloodline. No one in Mrs. Bartle's family could ever be a jerk.

"I'm sorry I never called you." What? Had he read her mind?

"Exactly how well do you two know each other?" Mrs. Bartle asked, her tone hinting that she might already be aware of the answer. Or perhaps she was just being playful. Barry fumbled with the reins.

"Uh...Diana is...was..." Barry spent a few moments searching for the most appropriate way to say *a girl I nailed during my pre-marital, pre-entrepreneurial stud days* before switching to a new approach. "We met at a...um...at...uh, well, the, uh...the house of a friend!" he finished lamely. It was a true answer, after all, and one that he thought would satisfy his ever-so-unintrusive auntie Rose.

"What friend?" Mrs. Bartle asked, raising her eyebrows. Obviously he hadn't visited Auntie Rose in a while. Diana, however, had a little more practice with her friend's bold, new Private I side, and Barry looked so cute and helpless that she knew a rescue mission was in order.

"The Suttons," Diana chimed in. "I used to baby-sit for their twins. And Barry and I met at a New Year's Eve party they had, oh, I guess it was about fifteen years ago." Barry nodded, looking so completely relieved and grateful that he made her want to continue rescuing him for as long as it took. "Barry," she proceeded, "was the Suttons' mechanic."

"Right. That's right," Barry said quickly.

"Right," Mrs. Bartle echoed, half skeptical and half amused. She always knew when Diana was covering something up. Maybe she was the same way with Barry. But as long as she didn't ask if her great-nephew had put a raincoat on his snake before he wandered into Diana's garden, they would all be fine. "Fifteen years ago, huh?" she asked, looking at Diana. "You must have been seventeen years old!" And this seemed to freak Barry out a lot more than the allegory of the condom would have.

"Se…se…seventeen?" he stammered, looking panicked.

"And William," Mrs. Bartle continued, "you were only twenty-eight. It's hard to believe you two even recognized each other now."

"Sev-en-teen?" Barry silently mouthed once Mrs. Bartle had turned away. Diana nodded at him coyly. It was funny how in fifteen years it had never occurred to her that the twenty-eight-year-old mechanic with the powder blue pickup truck may have thought she was older than jailbait when he lay down with her in the truck.

"But then again," Mrs. Bartle resumed, looking from one startled face to another, "New Year's Eve can get pretty wild."

"Tell me about it," Diana blurted. And then, in a terribly embarrassed attempt to pretend she hadn't, she began to cough wildly, hoping to erase her words from their memories with the distraction. In Mrs. Bartle's case, it seemed to work.

"Are you all right, dear?" she asked. "William, why don't you go get her a glass of water?" But Barry just stood there, staring at Diana with an adorably goofy smile on his face that signified either sheer nervousness or sheer amusement—Diana couldn't tell which. "William, she's turning blue," Mrs. Bartle pleaded. And, suddenly, Barry's smile disappeared, and with a serious nod, he turned toward the kitchen. Once he was gone, Diana artfully allowed her coughing fit to subside into a light clearing and patting of the throat, eventually sighing to indicate that it was all behind her. Mrs. Bartle kept quiet until the performance was over. "You never forgot him, huh?" she asked once normalcy had been restored.

"Nope," Diana said calmly, staring into space like she was staring at a dream, painted on some canvas a thousand miles away. And for a moment, it didn't even matter that Mrs. Bartle hadn't bought her performance. She was remembering that night in the truck, their night.

"Well, it seems he never forgot you, either," Mrs. Bartle said. "I mean, I've been in grocery stores and shopping malls with him when the girls would come up. He's been cursed at, slapped even. Although *they* were always the ones who ran off in tears."

"Mrs. Bartle, what on earth are you talking about?" Diana asked, flung back into the reality of the moment by her confusion.

"Oh, Diana, grab a clue!" her friend exclaimed, hitting her lightly on the shoulder. "I'm saying you must have been special. William hardly ever remembers the women he slept with in his bachelor days. He was quite the stud, you know."

Diana felt like she was about to faint. She couldn't believe how much this old woman knew—how much she was able to figure out just by watching, how well she understood their bizarre behaviors, loved them anyway, pardoned old indiscretions. But Mrs. Bartle always knew everything. More incredible was how cool she'd played it in front of Barry, who upon returning with the glass of water, stood frozen in the entryway, gripping it tightly in his hand.

"Thank you, William," Mrs. Bartle said, taking the glass from him like he was a fragile little boy playing "waiter," and she didn't have the heart to break *his* by letting him know how terrible he was at it.

Diana gulped the water down as only one who'd been stranded in the desert for two days could, made an excuse about resting up for work, and bolted as fast as her feet would carry her out of the living room that had just housed the singular most thrilling and embarrassing moment of her entire life.

June 21st

Dear Diary,

 Five more pounds—gone! I can't believe I'm back in the 160s! (167 to be exact.) This brings my total weight loss to eleven pounds! Only 37 more to go! My body aches constantly from the aerobics classes (I wonder if this is what toned people feel like all the time?)... Anyway, what an exciting week! It's funny how one's life gets exciting as soon as she decides it's going to be. Of course, the biggest thing was running into Barry (Ahem, I mean, WILLIAM BARRON. I still can't get used to that!). It's a scene I am convinced belongs in a movie (Who would play me, I wonder? I guess I'd have to lose all 37 remaining pounds before I could even pitch the idea to Hollywood, or else they'd cast someone who always plays "the fat, homely, but humorous woman" to play me.). I can't be-

*lieve I finally saw him again after all these years. I won-
der if he thought I looked good or bad. Of course, seeing
Barry again was not the only exciting thing that happened
to me this week. I also got the job at Happy Start and
gave Mick my two weeks' notice. And get this: he was actually nice about it. He said he was happy for me, and he
even looked kind of sad (although in retrospect, I'm thinking he probably just had acid reflux or something). Even
better, he said I only have to stay one more week instead
of two. This was after I told him I'd be moonlighting the
second week because that's when the camp starts. He said
not to bother because then I'd be too tired my first week at
the camp and would probably get fired and wind up back
at the diner again anyway. I can't believe I'm finally gonna
be rid of that place!… Oh, Scott's tonight! I nearly forgot
to mention the most important thing of all: I'm going to
have SEX with Mr. Wonderful before morning comes. I
mean, hey, if I can take an exercise class with Mom, stand
face-to-face with Barry after all these years, and quit Blue
Horizon, how hard could getting a guy at a bar to sleep
with me be? (Even if he is the hottest guy that ever lived.)
Luck to me!*
Diana

CHAPTER TWENTY-4

There he was. Playing pool as usual. Except for some reason, he didn't seem as intimidating as usual. Probably because Diana was wearing a size fourteen. Granted, it was a little snug, but not *Somebody-stepped-on-my-oxygen* snug. And she knew it was all right to admit to herself the snugness of things because she was already in a smaller size. It was acceptable snugness, snugness she understood to be temporary. However, if during her 178-days, her sixteens had felt a little snug, she would have convinced herself that she was either premenstrual *(Well, I* am *due in twelve days.)* or in need of a new washing machine *(That damn piece of crap shrinks everything I own!).* And this was because she would never have allowed herself to graduate to an eighteen. Of course, that was how she'd felt about sixteens before she'd graduated to those. But that was going

way back—Diana hadn't been a fourteen since the first
Bush administration. So, sitting here now, in a long, somewhat fitted, but not unflatteringly tight, black, V-neck,
size-fourteen dress—cleavage popping, hair fluffy, and
lips pouty—she couldn't feel more accomplished. Well,
actually, she could. But bedding Mr. Wonderful would
have to wait until after last call, or at least until he stopped
playing pool long enough to approach the bar for a drink.
For Diana had decided on no more pool compliments.
She was not about to risk utter humiliation for another
"Yeah, thanks."

   So she waited. And her thoughts turned to her reunion
with Barry in Mrs. Bartle's living room. She couldn't believe that for all these years he never knew she was only
seventeen that night in his pickup. But now that he knew,
his image of the girl he nailed during his premarital, pre-
entrepreneurial stud days—and actually *remembered*—
might be way sexier (once he was over that whole
robbing-the-cradle thing). For wasn't seventeen the quin-
tessential age of innocence and eroticism—ripe physical
maturity combined with childlike mystique, evenly
blended and equally obvious? Wasn't that what made seventeen the age of all those legendary teen queens im-
mortalized in pop songs? "(She's) Sexy + 17," the Stray
Cats. "I Saw Her Standing There," the Beatles. "Seventeen," Winger. Yes, Diana could not hide from the truth.
Despite the fact that for fifteen years, whenever she'd
think about Barry, which was often, she'd always picture
herself as a fumbling fatty—unsexiness oozing out by the
truckload—and assume that was how he remembered her

also, it was now quite apparent that she was a bit of a sex goddess back then and that, in light of the whole seventeen revelation, Barry was likely to become even more smitten with her memory.

"Excuse me." A voice suddenly interrupted her thoughts, causing Diana to lean away, afraid that if her upper body had been blocking some man's road to intoxication, she might not be as svelte as she thought. "Whoa! I didn't think I smelled *that* bad," the man said with a friendly laugh.

"What?" Diana asked, a little caught off guard, only to look up and be a *lot* caught off guard: it was *him!* Mr. Wonderful had been having a conversation with her, and she hadn't even known it. And here he stood now—facing her—with his right elbow on the bar, just centimeters from her own. His eyes were hazel.

"You moved kind of far away there," he said. And then he smiled. *Wow.*

"Sorry," Diana said, smiling back without even pausing to analyze whether or not smiling back was a good idea. Her heart was pounding. But it wasn't nerves. It was as if she'd been waiting her entire adult life for this moment, for this prelude to another one-night stand. And here she was, feeling that moment unfold—watching it, almost like it wasn't even happening to her. And she wanted to savor every thousandth of a millisecond. She wanted to memorize it—every blink, every smile, every heartbeat. But at the same time, she couldn't wait to see what would happen next. And after keeping a lid on her lust for so long, she wanted next to be *now.*

"It's okay," he said. He was staring at her. He had five o'clock shadow and a piece of white fuzz on his eyebrow. Diana thought about how corny it would be if she reached to remove it—like in a PG-13 romance when one soon-to-be-lover reaches over with her thumb to wipe mustard or a bread crumb off the mouth of the other and their eyes lock poignantly before moving in for the kiss. Besides, she didn't know him well enough to touch his eyebrow yet, which was kind of funny considering that she planned on seeing him naked before the sun came up. "I didn't need you to move at all, though," he continued. "I actually just wanted to give you this." What was it? His phone number? His high school ring? His first baby tooth?… Her sweater. It had fallen off the back of her seat. Not as exciting an offering as she'd hoped, but a chivalrous gesture nonetheless. Maybe this guy would actually stick around for tea and crumpets after the wad of tissues disappeared.

"Thanks," Diana said.

"No problem," he said, turning to face the bartender as he raised his beer bottle. "Hey, can I get another one of these?"

Was that it? Was that the end of the mating ritual? Did this guy really think her great expectations would be met with a sweater return and a "No problem"? *All right, Mr. No Problem,* Diana thought, *let's see what you do when I turn away from you.*

"What are you drinking?" *Oh, so you did notice! You noticed and now you want me back… Okay, done.*

"Um…" Shit. What was she drinking?

"Had a few too many?" he joked.

"Lager," Diana suddenly remembered, proudly adding, "draft," in hopes that the specification would detract from her brief moment of idiocy and make her appear knowledgeable. For even though this guy could clearly see on his own that she'd been drinking from the taps, due primarily to the fact that she had a glass in front of her instead of a bottle, overcompensation—in this case, providing excess information in response to an inquiry so as not to appear completely drunk and foolish—was still a more functional way of handling embarrassment than bolting red-faced from the room, knocking over chairs and people along the way. And being functional was Diana's new thing.

"And one lager draft for the lady…whose name is…?"

"Diana."

"Diana," he repeated, making her name sound sexier than sex. And then there was silence. Not the awkward kind of silence in which one can't think of a single appropriate word to say, but rather the savory sort of silence in which two strangers want to get it on so badly that words are a waste of energy. It was one of those meaningful and sweaty kinds of silences that usually precede graphic sex scenes in the movies.

"Travis." But it was short lived.

"Excuse me?" Diana asked. In the smoldering haze of seduction, she'd forgotten her senses, and it took her a moment to realize that "Travis" was most likely short for *My name is Travis.* "Oh hi," she giggled, making the connection before he could answer, and banking on cuteness to spare her from looking like a two-time idiot.

"Hi," he said, smiling as his eyes grazed over her chest. He didn't look like a Travis. He could have passed for a Jason, a Dylan, a Todd. Maybe even a Tyler. But not a Travis. Although he was more of a Travis than a Bob, Billy or Jack. "But don't ever call me that."

"What do you mean?" Diana asked.

"I mean 'Travis,'" he answered, suddenly looking quite serious. "Don't ever call me that." What was *this*? He'd told her his name but never wanted to hear her say it? Had it all been too good to be true? Had starting this conversation with her been nothing more than some ridiculously inverted way of saying *I'm not interested, so stop pining for me?* Was she about to be humiliated? "Call me TJ instead," he continued. "The only person who ever calls me Travis is my grandmother."

"Your grandmother?" Diana was so relieved, she had to consciously refrain from falling to her knees in the middle of the bar to thank God.

"Yeah. And you wouldn't want to be like her. She's really moody and has no teeth." He paused, inspecting her suspiciously until she smiled. "Well, now, I can see *you've* got teeth. But as for the moody part, I'd have to get to know you better." Was that an invitation?

"I'd like that," Diana said. What was she doing? The bold words dripped from her Malibu Pink lips before she could even think to calculate their potential to backfire.

"So would I." And, obviously, there was no need for calculations! Now *this* was not supposed to happen to women like Diana. Wait. Yes, it was. It was. It was. It was. She had to keep reminding herself that she deserved

Travis-but-don't-ever-call-me-that's attention. TJ. What a name. What a guy. She couldn't *believe* how close she was to getting him into bed.

"TJ!" a disruptive male voice suddenly called from behind them. "You comin' back or what?" Who was this schmuck—this rash intruder who thought he had the right to steal such a magical moment away from her? He approached the two of them like what they were sharing was trivial compared to pool, ignoring Diana like she was merely a piece of barroom kitsch that had distracted TJ from the art of the game. "Come on, dude! Will said he could kick my ass. You play winner." *Well, obviously, you couldn't play "winner,"* Diana silently snapped, *because you are a total LOSER who thinks it's completely acceptable to step on other people's most critical and forever-awaited moments, you stupid bastard. Come on, TJ,* she begged, *get rid of him.*

"All right, let's go," TJ said, moving away from the bar. "See ya, Diana." And he and the stupid-loser-bastard were both gone.

See ya Diana? That was it? After all they'd been through, that was all she was worth? They'd almost had SEX, for Lord's sake, and all she'd gotten was a "see ya"? Did she not have the words "Good Time" practically scrawled across her cleavage in pre-intimate perspiration? Had she not been pushing sex appeal all night? Sex appeal that TJ had seemed to clearly pick up on? What had happened to make him drop her so suddenly like a fat, smelly shoe? At least Barry had *feigned* concern for her well-being after they'd done it by telling her to get inside before she caught a chill. But TJ didn't seem to care how cold he had left her. What a prick.

"Hey." The prick was back. "Don't you go anywhere," he said. And there was something forceful and unmistakably erotic in his command. Diana watched him join his friends at the pool table and used the alone time to spend a few minutes thanking God that she'd shaved her legs and bikini line. Warm spasms of anticipation erupted in her stomach. There was no going back now—Diana was about to get lucky.

"Hold on. Let me get the lights," Diana said, groping her way toward the light switch as TJ groped his way up her dress. His hands had been all over her since they'd left the bar—in the parking lot, in her car, on the way into her apartment building, on the stairwell… It had been nonstop, over-the-clothes fondling the entire time. Diana knew he was a little intoxicated, but reassured herself that he seemed sober when he'd first begun hitting on her. So, even though alcohol may have intensified his desire, she reasoned it hadn't driven him to it.

"No, don't get the lights," TJ whispered, knocking into her plant stand and sending a huge ceramic flowerpot crashing to the floor. "Did I break it?" He panted—like someone pretending to care.

"No. I mean, maybe. But it's all right," Diana said, at-

tempting a sultry bedroom voice. Though a little embarrassed by her inability to find sexy words to console him
with, she was still quite impressed by how much she
sounded like Ginger from *Gilligan's Island*.

Diana led TJ to the bedroom, gripping at the walls to
keep her balance. Once inside, he started to tug at the
sides of her dress, which, being a snug fourteen now
clinging to beer bloat, was going to be a lot harder to take
off than it had been to put on. Crap. With all of the
primping and hair removal and shopping and seduction
planning, she'd never stopped to consider the stripping
aspect of sex. The dress was now bunched up around her
waist, exposing her control-top ass to the world of spec-
tators cheering by her bedside. Giving up on the dress,
TJ began kissing her. And, oh *God,* did it feel good to kiss
a man. He slid his hands slowly up the back of her stock-
ing-covered thighs and rested them gently on her rear
end. But as the kissing grew rougher, he began to squeeze.
At first, it was just a couple of squeezes, here and there,
like a man who liked big butts and was unabashedly fond
of hers. But then a rhythmic sequence of alternating
cheek squeezes emerged, as if he were a pornographic
baker kneading a giant pile of dough and getting off on
it. And somehow, although she was embarrassed to admit
it, even to herself, being TJ's giant pile of dough felt nice.

The room was absolutely pitch-black. Perfect nudity
lighting. And Diana wanted to be naked. She knew TJ
wouldn't be able to see her, and the whole experience
would just feel so much sexier if she were naked. But TJ
was obviously not up on his snug size-fourteen dress-re-

moval skills. But then again, how was he supposed to know that Diana needed to have her arms *inside* of the dress with her right shoulder stretched backward and consistently wiggling as she shimmied it upwards to her neck before the damn thing could finally be pulled over her head? After all, he was *only* a guy—a guy who was probably accustomed to having sex with waify super-model types who couldn't even *count* as high as fourteen. It was time to take matters into her own hands and squirm her way out of the dress, which she did as gracefully as possible. TJ followed her lead, pulling off his T-shirt and slipping Diana's bra straps off of her shoulders. He began sucking on her neck as he reached to unhook her bra. Cupping her breasts in his hands, he allowed his mouth to wander downward. Diana let her head fall back, and the room throbbed with an ecstasy she'd only read about in steamy novels. This was the stuff her hottest fantasies had been made of.

He was now stroking her inner thigh, traveling closer and closer to that hungry territory whose screams for affection were almost audible in the night. *Touch me,* Diana silently begged. What was he waiting for? *Ooh!* There it was.

Shivers danced through her body, making her knees shake and every untoned part of her body quiver—her thighs, her stomach, her butt, and especially her breasts, which, unlike those of the scrawny waifs TJ was probably used to dating, were one-hundred-percent real. She felt so incredible that nothing else in the world mattered. Only this unspeakable pleasure that she knew she'd never quite forget and never quite fully remember. If only she could bottle this feeling, she'd be the richest woman in the world. The underwear *had* to come off.

Pulling at the sides of her panty hose, she tried not to disturb the master at work. But TJ was obviously eager to continue the job with his master*piece* fully unveiled, for he pushed Diana's hands away, yanking both her stockings and underwear to her ankles in one clean motion. As she stepped barefoot onto the carpet, Diana had never felt more liberated, more sexual or more alive.

"I need to have a look at you," he said.

"What?" Diana whispered, opening her eyes. She'd heard him, but his words hadn't fully registered in her brain. And suddenly, the room was filled with light. Cold, sharp, glaring, invasive light that made her eyes water. TJ stood there staring. Diana didn't know whether to be mortified or turned on. She felt violated in a strangely arousing way—like she was starring in her own *I-accidentally-went-to-school-naked* dream, and the principal, played by TJ, was about to spank her for it. But then she caught a glimpse of herself in the mirror, and the naughty adult video in her mind became the absolute farthest thing from it—a deep crimson gash, left from the grip of her control tops, encircled her stomach. Now she knew why in the movies, they always wore garter belts. With the exception of the hideously unsexy battle scar she'd never really stopped to notice after past panty hose removals—a marking that clearly indicated an unresolved war with her weight—Diana knew this naked body a little *too* well to not suddenly feel panic and dread at the reality of someone else—*especially* the man of her dreams—standing in the same room with it, with the lights on and his eyes open. She wanted to run, but feared the jiggling-thigh-and-bouncing-butt syndrome that would probably result if she did. And so she just stood there—frozen—searching his face for any signs of rejection she could find.

But there were none. All TJ did was lick his lips and smile. Diana felt the blood returning to her body—she was back in the game. And soon the light grew endearing, as she ran her finger down her chest, staring confidently into TJ's eyes to let him know how ready she was. He moved toward her, unzipping his pants along the way. And then he was naked. And his body brushed up against hers as their eyes locked even more intensely. The condom wrapper was noisy, but neither of them were the slightest bit fazed by it, and it wasn't an awkward moment at all. It was just right, sweet, tender even. He kissed her softly on the mouth as she walked backward to the bed. And then he was on top of her.

It hurt more than she remembered. But the discomfort was more than tolerable—she liked it. Maybe this was what John Cougar Mellencamp had meant when he sang "Hurts So Good." Or maybe not. John Cougar Mellencamp had never had sex with TJ. But *she* had. And right now, at this very moment, no matter what else happened in her life, Diana would be able to say, with absolutely no embellishment whatsoever, that she'd had sex with her Mr. Wonderful. And that they'd done it in an actual bed—just like she'd always wanted.

"What's his name?" asked a coy Mrs. Bartle as she poured Diana a cup of tea.

"Whose?" Diana inquired innocently, though inside she was marveling at her friend's relentless ability to know absolutely everything.

"The boy who put that smile on your face. It wasn't there on Friday."

"Oh, *him*," Diana giggled. "His name is TJ, well Travis, actually, except no one ever really calls him that... His friends call him TJ."

"Miss Diana, do you have a boyfriend?" Mrs. Bartle asked, assuming her best Southern drawl and absolutely glowing at the prospect that the answer might be yes.

"Well, I don't know if I'd call him my *boyfriend* but—"

"He's special," Mrs. Bartle finished simply—and fortunately. For how could Diana explain their relationship without referring to the sex part?

The truth was that she didn't know what was going to happen with TJ. He'd passed out after they'd done it, and Diana had spent nearly an hour watching him sleep, only to find him gone when she awoke in the morning. She wasn't bothered by this, however. She hadn't expected him to spend *any* time there after they had sex, so whatever time he *had* spent was to be viewed as a bonus. Besides, after she had quit watching TJ sleep and had turned the lights off, she couldn't help but lay awake staring at a ceiling she couldn't see and agonizing over how in the world she'd be able to act sexy in the morning. On soap operas, couples were always waking up in bed and kissing right away, seeming equally as passionate as they were in the nighttime scene a few minutes before, and leaving Diana to wonder if either of them might have morning breath or those crusty eye particles that sleep makes. Perhaps portraying these perfect-looking people—the ones with the perfect bodies, perfectly contrived "bed-head" hairdos and picture-perfect makeup that remains flawless through an entire night's sleep (even on the men)—as also having perfect, round-the-clock wonderful breath and perfectly crust-free eyes was just another way that Hollywood screwed with people like Diana's self-esteem. She had never discussed it with the rest of the non-celebrity world, but she assumed she was not the only person on earth who found it appropriate to brush her teeth in the morning before breathing on other people. These were the thoughts that had kept her awake while

TJ slept. What if he should roll over in the morning and want to have sex again before she had a chance to brush and groom? What if, God forbid, he didn't try anything right away and they actually had to *talk*—in the sober and unforgiving light of day? Diana was definitely relieved that he hadn't stayed the night. Although, in spite of herself—she hadn't expected anything to actually come out of it; that's why they called them one-night stands—she was still a little disappointed not to find a note or a flower on the pillow next to her when she awoke. And she was embarrassed by her disappointment, knowing full well that she and TJ weren't Juliet and Romeo, Guinevere and Lancelot, or even Wilma and Fred. They were two people who'd had sex. Why should he have gotten all 17th-century poetic about that? Why was she? After all, TJ had been infinitely more gentlemanly than Barry. Barry. All roads led back to Barry. Why was that? Now that she'd had sex again, why hadn't the less-than-forty-eight-hours-old afterglow from her incredible night with TJ totally obliterated her fifteen-year-old memories of what, looking back now, was merely a mediocre night with Mrs. Bartle's great-nephew?

She couldn't stop comparing. And worse yet, her memories of the first moments of 1988 were playing tricks on her. For the face of twenty-eight-year-old Barry had been replaced by the face of Barry the entrepreneur, while the schoolgirl in the back of the pickup truck had matured into a thirty-two-year-old assistant-camp-counselor-to-be who was losing weight. Okay, so maybe Barry *had* grown up to be a decadently handsome middle-aged man, but he wasn't TJ. He wasn't so freakishly sexy that his looks could only be attributed to a miracle of nature. He didn't have that mysterious aura that made him seem too good for mortals. Talking to him didn't make her feel like if she could only move, she could fly. Barry had known the Suttons and had been divorced. TJ was a white knight, a living fantasy that had been in her bed. And from time to time while he was inside of her—while she was having sex with this touchable dream—she would hear Paul McCartney under her pillow singing with John, George and Ringo of a seventeen-year-old girl whose looks were way beyond compare.

"William says hello," Mrs. Bartle said suddenly, interrupting the quiet. Diana nearly choked on her tea. "He was quite surprised to see you last week," her friend continued nonchalantly, as if the incident had merely been a funny little coincidence and not some sort of frighteningly bizarre fate flub that wouldn't stop haunting her—not even when she was doing it with the sexiest man alive. It wasn't like she was in love with Barry or anything. She'd never loved Barry, not even for half a minute when she was seventeen. But he'd been in her mind since then, standing as the sole source of redemption for a lonely life of overweight celibacy. Whenever she'd think that no man could ever possibly want her, she'd remember: *Barry wanted me.* Whenever her mother would nag about her endless lack of male suitors, she'd remember, *Barry went after me,* and smile at the recollection of how upset Mrs. Christopher had been about that. But now, now that she wasn't the insecure, self-bashing, face-stuffing sack of lethargy she'd been since before she'd even met Barry, now that she'd turned her life around, lost eleven pounds, and set her sights on a fantasy she'd actually conquered, he was back?

"I was really surprised to see him, too," Diana said.

"You don't say?" Mrs. Bartle teased. Diana smiled and silently vowed not to let any information slip about what had happened between them. Her friend seemed to have already intuitively grouped her amongst Barry's long line of conquests, though as one of the special ones he actually remembered, from his studly run as a Baltimore bachelor. Something in their reunion—his apology, their shared nervousness, perhaps even a slight spark between them that only an outsider could see—had led her to draw this conclusion, and it made the mention of his name very awkward. Diana didn't even want to consider how awkward things could get once she knew the details. "May I ask you something, dear?"

Diana's heart began to accelerate. "What is it?"

"Was it your first time?" Mrs. Bartle's tone was gentle as she tilted her head sideways—very much in the empathetic fashion of a middle school guidance counselor. Honoring her personal vow not to discuss it, but refusing to lie to her best friend, Diana simply nodded—shyly and guiltily, like a little girl confessing her culpability in taping the "kick me" sign to Jimmy's back.

"It's okay, dear. I'm not going to make you sit in the corner for a 'time out.'" Mrs. Bartle paused, searching for the right words of wisdom. "Look, you're both good kids. And you were just *babies* back then…although

William was a bit disturbed to find out just how *much* of a baby you really were!" Mrs. Bartle laughed, and then, becoming serious, she continued. "Diana, don't let one night that happened fifteen years ago prevent you from making a good friend now. He's decided to move out here, you know. And I think the three of us could have a blast together." The crazy part, aside from her ninety-three-year-old friend granting her absolution from post-sex awkwardness, was that Diana knew she was right. If she and Barry were two of Mrs. Bartle's very favorite people in the world, how could the three of them *not* share a special chemistry and have an amazing time together?

"So, he's decided to move out here, huh?" Diana asked. "Can we expect the first Carr's Auto Repair on the East coast to be in Baltimore?"

"You've got it." Mrs. Bartle smiled proudly. "Now that his divorce is final…" She paused, looking upset. "I tell you, Diana, that woman did nothing but whine, run around and spend his money for eight years. We all knew she wasn't good for him—well, not at first. At first, she had us pretty fooled. My brother, Norman, and I were just so happy that after all those crazy bachelor years, the kid was finally settling down! And she seemed like a nice enough girl. Very pretty…a little on the skinny side, but pretty. And everything seemed wonderful at first. But then, after about six months, I'd start getting the late night phone calls, and William would be all sorts of upset because they'd had an argument and Jennifer still wasn't home yet or because Jennifer had maxed out yet another credit card and *still* wouldn't get a job—" Mrs. Bartle stopped suddenly.

"What's the matter?" Diana asked.

"I hope I'm not boring you, dear." *Boring* her? Was she kidding? Diana was fascinated by Barry and Jennifer. It was wild to realize that this guy who had taken her virginity and sped off without a trace in the earliest hours of 1988 had actually lived a life—outside of her head— after that. Besides, her years of feasting on talk show traumas had rendered her easily intrigued by other people's problems.

"You're not boring me at all!" Diana blurted eagerly. "I mean, um, please go on." Mrs. Bartle smiled. She was on to Diana and knew she was relishing the gossip.

"Well, as you can see, they really had their share of problems from the beginning, and none of them were William's fault. Jennifer came from a wealthy family and was accustomed to being spoiled. But when William tried to spoil her, when he tried to make her happy—well, it just wasn't good enough… The girl had gone to college for French Literature. Now I don't know *what* one does with a degree in French Literature, but this girl had one and did nothing but shop on Rodeo Drive, go to the gym and consult with her stylist. She was always spending money. Never worked a day in her life… Anyway, William was always working to support her, leading Jennifer to endlessly complain that he was never around. So, the 'poor, lonely thing' ended up having an affair. William was just devastated when he caught her. He came out here to stay with his parents for a while… But then Jennifer apologized and cried and sucked her thumb, and he eventually took her back. That's just the way William is.

Family is so important to him. And Jennifer *was* his family. He really wanted to hold on to that, no matter how much work was needed. And things really did seem better for a little while. But then when William's grandfather had his stroke, well..." Mrs. Bartle cleared her throat, choking back old tears. "I'm telling you, Diana, that boy flew out here every single weekend for nearly three months while Norman hung on. But did his 'loving' wife accompany him even *once?* No. Fine. We could live with that. But when William told us she wouldn't be attending the funeral because it conflicted with a liposuction she couldn't *possibly* reschedule...well, that was the final straw for all of us. And don't even ask me what part of her body she was having the fat sucked out of!"

"Oh, where, Mrs. Bartle? Where?" Diana asked, knowing her friend was just dying to tell.

"Her butt!" Mrs. Bartle exclaimed, laughing. "I mean, could you imagine?" Actually, Diana could. But she wasn't going to tell Mrs. Bartle that. "This girl was a size four, tops. But apparently, all the working out and screwing around in the world—pardon my language—was not going to give her the behind she wanted. And by not going to Norman's funeral, she basically chose her ass over William."

"Mrs. Bartle!" Diana was surprised. She'd never thought she'd see the day when sweet, old Mrs. Bartle would use the word "ass."

"Well, it's true, my dear," Mrs. Bartle said, smiling. "And William almost ended it with her after that. But she knew all the right buttons to push so he'd stay. He'd never lost anyone so close to him before, and he was grieving pretty badly. And Jennifer was there for him. I'll give her that. Although I can't be sure of what her motives were, I'll give her the fact that she was there for him. He liked to tell me in letters how sweet she was being. I'll never forget the one where he wrote, 'I've made a new best friend—one who even washes my clothes and makes sure I've had enough to eat even when I say I'm not hungry...' It broke my heart. Because I knew she'd go back to her old ways as soon as William was back to *his* old self again. And it's hard to watch someone you love get set up to take that kind of a fall... But I didn't want to bring him down. And, besides, I had no proof. So, I just kept my mouth shut and prayed for the best. And when the best didn't happen—as we all knew it wouldn't—William stood up to her, for the first time in his life.

"See, Jennifer was never very good at hiding her affairs. He'd already caught her once. And he'd suspected her many times after that. It always made him feel guilty—being suspicious of his own wife. But how could he not be? Once you've lost your trust in someone, they have to earn it back, and I don't know that Jennifer ever did. But I never wanted to reinforce his fears by telling him he had a *right* to be doubtful of her. As far as proof went, she'd been faithful since her 'one mistake,' as she so eloquently phrased it. But after her saint streak as the mourner's wife ended..." Mrs. Bartle sighed, rolling her eyes. "I'll give her credit. The act lasted longer than any of us thought it would. But when she dropped it, she dropped it, and she picked her old habits right up again.

William threw himself into his work for a while and didn't bother much with the situation at home. But then his suspicions began to gnaw at him, though not for the same reasons as before. It seemed he had finally realized that he deserved better, that he could *do* better than a spoiled brat wife who ran around. But it wasn't until he caught her in the act with the furniture deliveryman on the brand-new couch he'd let her order for their eighth wedding anniversary that he actually said it was over. Poor little Jennifer was devastated, as if the news had come out of nowhere. The family, however, we all wanted to throw a Hallelujah Party, but figured that would be insensitive. Anyway, they were separated for ten months while her daddy's lawyers haggled over the paperwork. And here he is. Well, actually, he's back in Los Angeles now on business. Poor thing. Traveling back and forth all the time like that. But he should be able to settle down out here for good in a few weeks."

A few weeks. So that gave Diana approximately twenty-one days to get over the weirdness of Barry rising from the ashes as the precious great-nephew Mrs. Bartle had known since his diaper days. After hearing about all he'd been through, Diana thought they might even have a shot at being friends. From the picture his great-aunt had just painted, Barry seemed like one of the kindest and most moral men in America. Too bad Diana seemed to have a thing for bad boys who didn't stick around.

"So, Diana, tell me about TJ," Mrs. Bartle said, changing the subject with a teasing smile. TJ? How could she

convey the fantastical magic that was TJ without including the impossibly romantic bedroom scene they'd
starred in?

"Well, I met him at Scott's Tavern over on Bridge
Street."

"Uh-huh…" Mrs. Bartle cooed, like she was about to
break into her own rendition of *Diana and TJ sitting in a
tree!* She knew there was a whole lot more to this story,
and she was waiting to hear it—all of it.

"Okay, actually, I spent two weeks pining over him before he even noticed me."

"Uh-huh…" *K-I-S-S-I-N-G!*

"Well, we finally got to talking on Saturday night,
and…well…one thing led to another and—"

"How was he?" Mrs. Bartle interrupted.

"Incredible!" Diana gushed. And for some reason, she
wasn't embarrassed. In fact, Diana was quite exuberant
about finally having a life to talk about and actually having someone she wanted to talk about it with. While she
did spare Mrs. Bartle the blow-by-blow of who un-
dressed who first and who kissed who where, she still
managed to make her friend understand the depth of de-
light beneath her smiling face. It was a happiness fifteen
years in the waiting and one miraculous, most perfect
night in the making.

Life was very good.

"For she's a jolly good fellow! For she's a jolly good fellow! For she's a jolly, good fell-ow! That nobody can deny! That nobody can deny…" As they all went on with their song—Mick, Brooke, the two night shift busboys, Julio and Curtis, and even Willie the cook—Diana couldn't believe they cared enough about her leaving to say anything more than goodbye. She hadn't expected much from her last night at Blue Horizon, except for maybe a *Your last paycheck is in the mail, so don't think I stiffed ya* from Mick. But when she'd walked into the kitchen for her very final break, there'd been a cake, a "Good Luck" balloon, and six wineglasses filled with milk. Diana would barely let herself admit it, now that after two years of blaming her life's misery on working there, she was finally getting out, but maybe Blue Horizon Diner wasn't the hell she'd always made it out to be. All of her life, she'd always constructed her own hell—her own safe, private little hell, cultivated from a personal gold mine of tragedy, disappointment and regret. Her apocalypse a few weeks ago with Mrs. Bartle—the major epiphany she'd experienced after the tumor blimp had proven itself too benign to carry her away—had taught her that she'd imprisoned herself in status quo misery for so many years to avoid taking chances. And all of the things that she'd once viewed as evil, loathsome, self-esteem-fucking wastes of time—this job, lunch with her mother, attempting to lose weight—no longer seemed dreadful or scary. But as far as her job went, she didn't *just* want to do something that didn't absolutely suck. She actually wanted to enjoy what she did, to love it, not just tolerate it. And that's why she was leaving. She wasn't running away—she was chasing happiness.

"We're gonna miss ya, Dee," Mick said when the crowd stopped singing. What was this? This wasn't the wise-cracking, *The-customer-is-always-right* and *You-don't-get-paid-to-daydream* boss who'd been a constant symbolic reminder of what a loser she'd for so long believed herself to be. This wasn't the guy who'd embarrass her for playing "beauty parlor" with the napkin dispenser and then joke that she had no one to impress anyway. Mick seemed genuinely sorry to see her go. "Now, ya don't have to say you're gonna miss us, too 'cause we know *that* ain't true," he continued. Diana laughed. "Come on, Dee, you could at least tell me I'm wrong!" Diana laughed again— she would do nothing of the sort. For even though the old place was turning out to be better than the hell hole she'd always thought it was, there was no way she could lie with a straight face about being sad to leave it. "Ah, to hell with all of ya's," Mick said. "I'm cuttin' the cake."

Diana's goodbye party only lasted another ten minutes, but it was a ten minutes guaranteed good for at least a week to replenish her self-perception whenever it needed a boost. Brooke asked to exchange e-mail addresses and said she would keep in touch. Willie told her he'd cook her anything she wanted free of charge anytime she stopped in, and that if Mick didn't like it, he'd hang up his spatula and leave. And Julio kept eyeing her, causing her to suddenly realize what a wealth of untapped sexual potential he had, untapped by *her* at least, which was probably fortunate considering that he was barely eighteen years old. But his attention was welcome regardless. However, the absolute best moment, hands down, came when Mick was slicing the cake and said, "Now, Diana's gettin' so skinny, I don't even know if she still *eats* cake." The sound of those words alone tasted better than any food Diana had ever gotten fat on, and so she celebrated with a piece of cake so little it didn't even count, and went home singing about what a jolly good fellow she'd actually turned out to be.

June 28th

Dear Diary,

Guess what? I got a new outfit today, and it wasn't at The Queen's Closet, but at Jillie's! As in a regular store where regular sizes shop. I went right in, tried on something I liked, and bought it, easy as anything. And it fits! Like really and truly fits—I don't feel pinched or poured in anywhere! So, naturally, I did my weekly weigh-in the second I walked through the door, and the scale said (drum-roll, please... Oh, I can't believe I'm about to write this number and won't even be lying!): 161! That's 17 pounds so far—just 31 more until I reach my goal weight. But then again, I hear that people set pretty unrealistic goal weights for themselves, so maybe I should raise mine ten, as not to become like one of those anorexic joggers I see from time to time running alongside traffic, bones jutting *out every which way but, still, their anxious, emaciated faces all twisted up over their legs still being bigger than the two plain celery sticks they ate for lunch. I don't want to become like that, so perhaps I should set 140 as my goal, and any weight I lose after that will seem like a present. Wait, what am I babbling about anorexic celery and unrealistic ideals for when I'm seeing TJ tonight, for Lord's sake? I mean, it's not like a date or anything wildly dramatic like that, but it's Saturday night, so I'll see him at Scott's. He'll recognize me because I'll be the one wearing the shiny, black, fake leather, size-fourteen pants that aren't too tight and the short-sleeved, burgundy, scoop-neck top. Oh, my God, I just had a shiver—I'm actually going to see TJ tonight! TJ, TJ, TJ, TJ, TJ! I cannot believe it's already been a week. Who would have guessed last week, when I was such a bundle of nerves to hit on him, that this week my skittishness would be over his seeing me dressed and out and about in society again after standing NAKED together with the lights on and having SEX in my bed? Oh God, this is too much to take! I feel like I could vomit…but in a good way.*

Diana

He didn't show. How was it possible that they'd shared such an amazing night together and he didn't even want to *see* her? Was he playing pool somewhere else? Why not at Scott's? Diana couldn't make sense out of it. She wished he'd left his phone number so she could call him. She wished she knew his last name. Maybe in fifteen years, he'd show up someplace freakishly coincidental and reveal it to her, just like Barry had done with Carr. But she didn't want TJ to be another Barry. She didn't want to lie awake dreaming of him until she was forty-seven years old. She wanted to lie *asleep,* dreaming *next* to him—*now.* Didn't he care about how sexy she was in her new, and completely comfortable, fourteen from Jillie's? Didn't he care that she'd lost six pounds since he'd last seen her naked and that she'd managed to do it *while* increasing muscle mass through aerobic exercise? Maybe he'd died. That was a possibility. After all, what did Diana know about his life? He could be a drag racer, a bullfighter, a stunt double or even a professional asshole that slept with women who worshipped him and routinely avoided them afterward. A butcher, a baker, a candlestick maker... oh, where the hell was TJ?

Diana wanted to burst into tears. She'd been at the bar since 10:15 waiting—waiting for a half-assed delusion to spontaneously come to life. Who had she been kidding? Did she really think that TJ was going to ride into Scott's Tavern on a white horse and whisk her away to a perfect life? Well, maybe not. But she *did* believe they'd shared something special, something he would at least want to rekindle after a few drinks on a Saturday night. What was wrong with her? Was she bad in bed? He didn't seem to think so, at least not while it was happening. But what if, in retrospect, he did? What if her fifteen-year gap in sexual experience had been evident and, worse yet, a turn-off? What if he were carrying around the mental image of Diana naked with stretch marks and a bright pink, control-top-panty hose gash encircling her stomach?

The fears ran wild in Diana's head. They were unstoppable. But even more troubling was her tremendous sense of failure. Everything had been going so well, and now this. What if this signaled the inevitable end that, as the saying goes, all good things must come to? What would happen then? Would everything good, all the wrinkles in her world that she'd finally ironed out—her weight, her mother, her job, her self-image—

would it all begin to slip away until the favorable order she'd longed for, and had finally managed to make real, was reversed? She didn't want to turn back into a 178-pound woman wishing on azaleas and searching the sky for blimps. Just the thought of returning to her old self and never knowing a thinner moment or what it was to like life again made her sick—sick enough to make her vow, *Never again.* As she downed the night's final sips of beer, Diana made herself a promise: *No matter what happens with TJ, I will not let myself get fat and pray for death. Regardless of whether he loves me, laughs at me, or never shows up in my life again, I'll continue to refuse the old Diana sunlight. Never again will I let her see the world.*

It was time to go by the time Diana realized she was drunk. She'd guzzled five beers during those torturous hours of waiting for nothing. Things had seemed fine while she was seated and, as she saw it, merely nursing her buzz with baby sips. *But four hours of baby sips make more than just a buzzed baby,* Diana thought. *They make a drunk mama.* Suppressing the urge to giggle out loud at her stunning inner wit, she made one last trip into the bathroom. She hadn't visited since beer number three when she was, in her opinion, sober, and judging by the way she bumped into practically every barstool on this final trip, it seemed that those last two beers were the ones that had pushed her over the edge. She didn't know how she was going to get home. Calling a cab was out of the question. It was just too shameful and sad. For to this day, and dating back more years than she could readily count, every time Diana saw an intoxicated person get out of a cab, she'd think of Bernie and want to cry.

Bernie was the neighborhood drunk of Diana's childhood. Between the ages of eight and ten, she was awakened nearly every night just after two by the sounds of a taxi door slamming, metal trash cans falling to the ground, and, in the warm weather when her bedroom window was open, Bernie belching and hiccuping his way to his mother's front porch, onto which he'd usually collapse, crashing down on the wooden boards like a comatose elephant. Diana had always found his solitary, stumbling shadow somewhat intriguing. But it wasn't until she'd heard Mrs. Christopher refer to him as "the lousy drunk three houses down who's thirty-five, unemployed, and still living with his poor, old mother" that she really began to take an interest in him.

Many days, she'd see Bernie sitting outside on her way home from school, and his empty eyes would follow her along the sidewalk as he sipped dark liquid from a brown paper bag. He didn't look so lousy to her, but rather like a portrait of the loneliest man in the world. One afternoon, she finally dared herself to wave. After all, everybody needed at least one friend. Perhaps, she could be his. To Diana's amazement, a smile actually stretched across his face, making his stubbly, sunken cheeks round and bringing a glimmer of light to his eyes. *See,* she had told herself, *all he needed was me.* Every day after that, Diana made a point of waving to the nice man that nobody understood and watching him, if even for a second, become a happier person for knowing her.

Lying in bed every night, awakened by the sounds of his homecoming, Diana created a life for Bernie, and it was a life filled with loneliness and more than one man's share of sorrow. For as she figured it, his mother was old and sick and a little out of her mind, his father was dead, he'd never had a wife, and drinking was the only way he knew how to dull the pain of solitude. After a while, she no longer waited to be lured out of sleep by his noisy arrival, but instead found herself purposely staying awake each night, just waiting to hear that cab door slam shut so that she could run to her window and make sure he got home okay. And despite the knocking into things and falling all over the place, he always did. Until one night, when he didn't.

Diana was ten when she watched Bernie trip over a dead bird and crack his head on the sidewalk. She was ten when she saw the blood spilling from Bernie's head, blood she tried to tell herself was from the bird, the same splattered bird that had been lying by the curb for nearly two days and couldn't possibly have had that much blood left to lose. But Diana couldn't bear for Bernie to hurt, and so the pain and the blood, and the terrible fear that must have been caused by both, just *had* to belong to the bird. With her hands held tightly over her ears—as if the sound of a bleeding man were too deafening to scream above—she'd yelled, "It's only bird's blood! Bird's blood! Bird's blood! Bird's blood!" until Mrs. Christopher awoke and raced into her daughter's bedroom, encircling her with the pink, fluffy sleeves of her bathrobe and shielding Diana's eyes. Diana had struggled with her mother that night, twisting violently and elbowing her in the stomach while yelling over and over again, "Let me go! You're killing him!" until the sound of the ambulance siren gave her the strength to knock Mrs. Christopher to the floor. She had then rushed downstairs, as fast as her trembling feet would allow her, arriving at the front door in time to see three paramedics carrying the stretcher away from the curb, their faces solemn but not nearly as sad as they should have been. For on top of the stretcher was a white sheet shaped like a man, with a bright red stain growing where the head was.

As Diana ran out of the house and into the street, she could hear her mother ten steps behind her, anxiously calling her name in a voice that begged her to come back inside. Diana reached the ambulance just in time to watch its doors slam closed on the only man she'd cared about since Daddy, a man whose life had just been extinguished because no one had ever reached out their hand to help him—not even when he was dying. She had begun to help him, but it hadn't been enough. She shouldn't have stopped at the waving. She should have talked to him, gotten to know him for real, seen if the life she'd created for him in her head was anything like the life he really led. She should have been a true friend. Now it was too late.

"NO!" Diana had screamed as the ambulance seemed to fade away in slow motion. And it was the loudest scream the town had ever heard. Maybe it was for her father. She'd killed him, too. But she'd been too young to fully understand what she'd done to Daddy. She'd never really learned the details of his accident. But she did know what she'd done to Bernie—she'd let him die. And that was just as bad as killing someone. She should've run out to help him *before* her mother woke up. Maybe, then, she could have saved him—that poor, misunderstood little man who'd never hurt anybody but himself.

Her scream spawned a united gasp, more startling than her desperate cry, and she turned to see an entire neighborhood staring at her, like she was some kind of possessed demon-child from a horror film. Not one of them put their arms around her or told her it would be all right. Middle-aged suburbia in their coordinated pajama sets and His and Hers bathrobes. The same people who had always rejected Bernie as an untouchable freak now looked at her the same way. The worst part was seeing Mrs. Christopher amongst them and recognizing that very same appalled look of rejection in her own mother's eyes, staring at her from the front porch like Diana was a stranger and no more a part of her than she was of anyone else in the neighborhood.

Diana had remained motionless after the ambulance disappeared, standing still for what felt like days, as she waited for her mother to come to her and take her back inside. But Mrs. Christopher never did. And all the other neighbors eventually tired of the freak show and went back to bed, leaving Diana alone in the street, staring at her mother, who eventually turned to go back inside herself. "Come on, Diana" was all she'd said. And with the exception of "You don't have to go to school today if you don't want to" the next morning at breakfast, Mrs. Christopher never so much as hinted at the subject ever again.

Bernie's mother, on the other hand, had slept through the entire thing and had died in that very same sleep by morning. The neighborhood had called it creepy, but Diana had figured that even in her sleep, his mother had somehow known what had happened and had finally allowed herself to die, having been ready for a long time but never wanting to leave Bernie all alone. She viewed it as a bittersweet ending to a terrible tragedy. She thought it was nice.

Diana definitely didn't want to be the town Bernie. She didn't need to pull up to her building in a cab in the middle of the night so that all the tenants could wonder about *her* life, assume it was pitiful, pass judgment on her, and when the time came, refuse to shed a tear for her death. She would just walk home and hope not to knock over any trash cans along the way. *I'll be fine* was all she had to keep telling herself. Well, that, and *TJ is an asshole.* The mantra kept her focused and carried her steadily homeward without any accidents.

Glen Vali Suites looked different after five beers, and so did the moon. It was as if *she* were normal, and everything around her—the moon, the stars, her building, and each jumbo, white, night-blooming flower on the vine that climbed the gate—was drunk.

"They're beautiful, aren't they?" A gentle voice penetrated the silent summer night, causing Diana to spin around nervously and crash right into the arms of the intruder.

"Sorry," she apologized, without looking up.

"It's okay." The voice was familiar. It was Barry.

"What are you doing here?" Mrs. Bartle hadn't said anything about him coming.

"Well, I figured you might need someone to catch you when a strange man's voice in the dark made you spin around and lose your balance."

"Oh, is that so?" Diana wanted to appear sober, so she thought it best not to attempt any witty responses of her own.

"No, actually it's not," Barry admitted. "I was just taking a walk."

"At two o'clock in the morning?"

"Well, actually it's almost three. Which gives *me* reason to return the inquiry." Barry leaned forward. "What are *you* doing here?"

"I live here."

"Are you in the habit of wandering around unaccompanied at 3:00 a.m.?"

"Well, what's your excuse?" Diana asked.

"I'm still on California time," Barry said. "It's not even midnight there yet."

"Ah," Diana returned, raising her eyebrows with an exaggerated nod.

"Good time at the bar tonight?"

His words hit her slowly. The atmosphere had begun to spin around her a bit, but aside from that, she thought she'd been hiding her earlier whereabouts rather well. "What makes you think I was at a bar?" she asked, sinking suddenly toward the ground.

"Whoa, I've gotcha," Barry said, putting his arms

around her as he helped her to the lawn. "By the way," he continued, whispering in her ear, "I hope you were better at stuff like this when you were a teenager."

"Better at stuff like what?" Diana squinted at him, confused. They were both seated on the lawn, facing the beautiful white flowers on the vine along the gate—the kind that opened at sunset and made the air smell sweeter than the most delicious dessert.

"I don't know," he laughed. "Better at coming up with reasons for why you were out walking at the very same time the bars close, better at covering up beer breath, better at *not* falling down. God, if I were your mother, I'd have been relieved to have a kid whose dishonesty was so transparent. I'd always know when you were lying to me."

"Like the way you 'knew' I was over eighteen?" Diana teased, closing her eyes and letting her head fall back a little.

"What?"

"Remember?" she asked, facing him. "That night in your truck? We went outside and it was cold—totally unlike tonight—and you led me over to your—"

"I remember," he interrupted. "But believe me, I wouldn't have done it if I'd known how young you were."

"I was *just* a little girl, Barry," Diana said, smiling, loving the game.

"I know that now," Barry said, his deep brown eyes piercing her with a sudden seriousness that, in the drunken moonlight by the flowers, made the moment seem intense, pivotal even.

"I was a virgin," Diana whispered, staring at him solemnly.

"I know," Barry admitted. "I mean, I didn't know…at first," he stammered. "But then I, uh…well, I felt something and I knew."

"You felt something?" What was it? A psychic broadcast announcing *This girl is a virgin?* An angel on his shoulder beseeching him to stop? An overwhelming urge to take her in his arms and protect her precious and until-then-totally-untouched chastity for the rest of their days?

"Blood," he said, his face cringing awkwardly.

"Oh, right." Duh. "I guess that was kind of a turn-off, huh?"

"No, not really," Barry said, looking down. "Quite the opposite, in fact."

"You mean it turned you ON?"

"You don't have to say it so loud," Barry protested lightly, keeping his eyes on the lawn. He was embarrassed; Diana could tell. In fact, if she were sober, and it weren't so dark outside, she'd know for sure that he was blushing. And even through her moonlit haze of inebriation, she found his fumbling sincerity endearing. After a few moments, he looked up. The seriousness had returned to his eyes. "I'm really sorry I never called you afterward."

"Barry, you didn't have my phone number."

"I'm sorry I never asked for it."

"You are?" Mrs. Bartle had been right about Barry Carr all along. He truly *was* a good guy.

"I was different then," Barry explained. "I was young

and stupid, as the saying goes… Diana, I was intimate with a lot of women. No. Intimate…intimate isn't the right word. I…" As Barry searched for a suitable euphemism for *had sex with,* one that wouldn't seem like a justification, Diana wondered if she should tell him that he had no reason to feel guilty over her, that even though the tissue thing after the climax of his performance had been a somewhat tacky way to end the show, she wasn't screwed up over what they had done, and she never had been.

She wanted to say, *Hey, you were the only man that had ever made me feel sexy. What we did was both the ultimate grand prize to end a shitty adolescence and the white knight of a very lonely adulthood. If you only knew how many times the memory of that one night has kept blood pumping through my veins, even when I've felt like the biggest, fattest loser on the planet— when I went through my entire twenties without ever once having sex, when my mother or Mick made me realize, through some supposedly harmless suggestion or joke, that I was a fat failure, when Dr. Mason explained the rarity of immaculate conception, and even when he scheduled my biopsy—if you knew how that night in your pickup truck made me forget the world and pray for passion, giving me a reason to think my life had possibilities and an emergency dose of self-esteem when I needed it, you'd realize that apologies now are beyond unnecessary. My father, my mother, and everyone I have ever known (with the exception, of course, of your brilliant and beautiful aunt Rose)—anyone else, including myself—could, and is welcome to, take the blame for what, up until a few weeks ago, was a not-so-wonderful life. Anyone except for you. You, who for one night broke up the monotony and made me feel like the most special person in the room in a way that no one had done before and no one had done since until…*

Crap. She'd managed to forget about TJ for a little while—in the fragrant air of summer flowers that only bloomed when the sun went down and in the company of her first fling who was doing such a good job of making her remember *their* magic—and now, here he was, Travis Whatever-the-Hell-the-"J"-Stands-For Last Name Unknown, intruding upon the non-depressingness of everything. What a bastard.

"I was a slut," Barry finally concluded. A strange confession for a man to make, but an admirably honest one nonetheless, and at least it had rescued her from another round of TJ-bashing, one that would have undoubtedly transformed itself into the evening's second *What-is-wrong-with-me?* marathon.

"A slut?"

"That's the only explanation I can give you."

"Barry, I don't need an explanation."

"But I do."

"What do you mean?"

"I mean, I was a slut. I slept with a lot of women, some of them married even, with absolutely no regard for how they felt afterward or for what it would do to their lives."

"Yeah, but Barry, these married women were the ones who were cheating, not you. I think you're being too hard on yourself." Seriously, Diana thought, what had the man done that was so awful? These married women were the ones breaking all their vows of loyalty and tampering with a life they'd created for themselves in front of God and

all of their relatives and friends. Barry had been a solo op-
erator, free to sleep with whomever consented, and not
guilty of coercion or betrayal when some married woman
decided to risk everything. Maybe the alcohol had
maimed Diana's objectivity, but she couldn't see what was
so bad about what he'd done.

"I slept with Clara Sutton." And there it was. Diana felt
like she'd just had the wind knocked out of her. Not Mrs.
Sutton. Not Sarah and Jack's mom. Not the woman
whose life Diana had spent her teenage years looking to
as a prototype for what a functional wife and mother
should be.

"Barry, you didn't! That's horrible! She had a family!"

"Well, so did these other women. And you just said I
was being too hard on myself about *them*," Barry said. But
Diana just stared at him, unsure of how to react. She
wasn't exactly mad at him, and truth be told, she didn't
really give a rat's ass now about Clara and Clifford Sutton's marriage and what happened to it back in the de-
cade of big hair and shoulder pads. It was more like…she
was jealous. "Do you forgive me?"

"Well, that depends," Diana said, trying to act playful
and unaffected. "Was it before or after me?"

"Which answer would get me off the hook?"

"I'm not sure, so just be honest."

"After." Now that she'd heard it, "after" was definitely
the wrong response. Diana knew Barry had been with
other women since her, but having a visual of one of them
definitely detracted from what now revealed themselves
as the complete delusions of grandeur she'd been having

ever since Mrs. Bartle said—and Barry's actions implied—that she was special. "And before."

"What?" Was he toying with her?

"We had an affair."

"An affair? As in long-term?"

"As in she's one of the two reasons I left Baltimore. I didn't go to Los Angeles just to start an auto body chain. I could've done that here. But I needed to leave, and Clara was one of the reasons why."

"What was the other one?" Diana asked.

"You."

"Me?" He was definitely toying with her.

"Between screwing up Clara's marriage and realizing you were a virgin—that both of you would remember me and what we'd done for the rest of your lives…well, I suddenly saw myself a little too clearly, and, needless to say, I didn't like what I saw."

"What did you see?"

"A man who used people and threw them away. Someone who messed up people's lives and moved on, without ever offering a hand in helping to put back together what I'd so selfishly—and thoughtlessly—torn apart."

"But, Barry, it wasn't like that with us. Don't you see? I was like *you*. I wasn't looking for anything more than you gave me. In fact, what you gave me was exactly what I needed, and I've never had any regrets." Diana could not believe how bold the night had made her. Here she was— on the brink of telling Barry how she'd really felt about him for the past fifteen years. "You were never like the guy you thought you were. At least not in my eyes."

"Well, that's very comforting to know," Barry said, grinning warmly. "But I'm glad I didn't have the consolation back then."

"Why is that?"

"Because I may have never changed. And then I might have never had the chance to tell you that you were special."

"I knew," Diana teased, letting her smile get as big as it wanted to.

"Oh, is that right?" Barry asked, shoving her playfully. Diana wanted so badly to ask him about his marriage, about Jennifer and how they had met, about what had made him think she was the one. But she felt greedy. Barry's whole middle-of-the-night gut-spilling session shouldn't have left her craving *more* dirt—the dirt he'd already given her should have been enough.

"What?" he asked suddenly, sensing in her silence that something was amiss. But Diana just shrugged, too embarrassed to ask about the *one* thing he hadn't divulged. "You're probably wondering how my divorce plays into all of this." Diana was amazed—the man *had* to be psychic.

"Actually, I already know about it," Diana said, playing it cool, not wanting to sound too eager. "Your aunt told me everything."

"Everything?" Barry asked, pretending to be impressed.

"Yes, everything," Diana answered haughtily, returning the sarcasm.

"Oh, okay. So I guess I don't have to tell you about Jennifer."

"Fine," Diana said, wondering how good she was at

pretending she wasn't dying of curiosity. Barry smiled to himself. Sitting with his knees to his chest, he harbored the devilishly smug expression of the playground know-it-all who claimed to know exactly how many licks it took to get to the center of a Tootsie Pop but wouldn't tell anyone.

"Oh, come on, tell me!" Diana suddenly burst out. Apparently, *she* was the kid on the playground who was too eager to realize that feigning disinterest was a surefire way of getting the secret-keeper to spill. After all, privileged information was only fun when it could be used to torture other people.

"Nope!" Barry said, remaining tight-lipped as he stared up at the stars above them. It seemed he was planning on torturing Diana for as long as he could hold out.

"Oh, come on. Don't tease me," Diana begged. But the truth was that she enjoyed it. She hadn't had such childlike fun since her father was alive. Barry's resistance reminded her of the way Daddy used to hold out on her, when he'd pretend he didn't know where he was taking her on their special day out or what flavor of ice cream he'd bought at the market.

"I'm not teasing," Barry explained. "I'm just wondering."

"Wondering what?"

"Why you never answered me."

"About what?"

"The flowers."

"What are you talking about?" Diana didn't know *this* game.

"The flowers right there," Barry said, gesturing toward the big, white flowers they'd been facing since Diana's loss of balance had sent the two of them to the ground.

"You never asked me about the flowers."

"Well, that shows what you know. I absolutely *did* ask you about the flowers." Barry leaned over, lowering his voice. "I was the stranger in the night who startled you."

"Oh, yeah," Diana said, remembering.

"Oh, yeah," Barry mimicked her.

"Well, fine, Mr. Carr, I'll tell you what I think of the flowers."

"I'm listening," Barry said.

"I think…" Diana didn't feel drunk anymore, just peaceful and uninhibited, with a clarity she'd never really possessed before. "I think," she continued confidently and with full conviction, "they're not as lovely as azaleas."

"Azaleas?"

"Yes, azaleas. These flowers are beautiful. But there are no flowers more magical or more powerful than azaleas."

"And why is that?"

Diana moved her face closer to Barry's in what was probably a subconscious attempt to protect the sacred nature of what she was about to disclose from any unsympathetic elements in the atmosphere that may have been lingering between them. "Azaleas brought my father back to earth," she whispered. Barry's face turned as serious as stone, and neither of them spoke until he broke into a smile and sighed, hanging his head in a charmingly self-imposed shame, like he was the last one at the party to get the joke.

"He was an astronaut," he said matter-of-factly, looking up again to meet Diana's curious stare.

"No, he was dead," Diana replied. Blazing with shock, Barry's bulging eyes appeared to be contemplating a jump from their sockets. "Well, he *is* dead," Diana continued. "He's… Did your aunt ever tell you about my cancer scare?"

"Your cancer scare? No. What happened? Are you all right?" All signs of amazement had disappeared from Barry's face, and the only thing evident was genuine concern. Diana wondered if it would be evil to pretend that maybe she wasn't all right, just so that she could hold on a little longer to this feeling of being cared about by a man. But she figured it was bad luck to play tricks where her health was concerned, and Barry was too nice of a guy to torment. So she decided to go with honesty.

"I'm fine."

"Oh, thank God," Barry said, putting his hand to his heart. It was a reaction she'd gift wrap and distribute for free to every woman in America if she could. It would come in so handy when all men seemed like unfeeling assholes who just didn't care, which, in many women's lives, was probably most of the time. Barry's response made her want to tell him everything.

"Anyway, it was a few weeks ago when my doctor said there might be a tumor in my fallopian tube," Diana began.

"A tumor?" Barry seemed frightened.

"Barry, I'm *okay,*" Diana said, reassuring him with her giant smile. "It turned out to be benign. But during my one day of not knowing, I went to sleep and dreamt the most beautiful dream."

"What was it about?"

"Azaleas."

"Azaleas," Barry repeated, as if the word had suddenly become its own island of mystical elegance, too sacred and wonderful not to be echoed.

"I was in a beautiful garden full of them, a garden that just radiated with their bright, pink color, when out of nowhere, a giant tumor blimp appeared in the sky."

"A tumor blimp?"

"Yeah, kind of like the Goodyear blimp but only with the word 'tumor' painted across it, instead. And my father was inside of it. He wanted me to pick some azaleas for him. He didn't say a word, neither of us did. But I knew that's what he wanted, so I gave him as many as I was able to hold in my hands, and…" Diana sighed, looking away and remembering how great it had felt to be with her father again. "We flew away on that blimp together."

"And then you found out it wasn't cancer," Barry said softly.

"And then I found out it wasn't cancer," Diana reflected, still looking away. After a few moments, she began to drift back into the present and started to worry that Barry might think she still had a death wish. She was thrilled that he had understood her in the first place, for she'd never intended to share that dream with anyone, not even Mrs. Bartle. But she didn't want him to think she was a suicide case or, in any sense, still suffering from delusions of blimps. Spinning around to face him, she broke the silence, announcing, "I'm lucky to be alive."

"Yes, you are," Barry agreed, guiding her head onto his shoulder. "We all are."

It felt wonderful to be held by a man. The world seemed like home, and everything felt safe and sweet. She wanted things to stay this way, for as long as they could.

"Tell me about your name."

"My name?"

"Mrs. Bartle has been talking about you for years," Diana explained. "Silly me, I never stopped to think her great-nephew, *William,* might have been the Barry I once knew."

Barry laughed, making Diana feel witty and adorable. "Well, Barry comes from my middle name, Barron."

"I kind of figured that."

"Hey, do you want me to explain this to you or not?" Barry asked, feigning offense.

"Sorry, please do."

"All right. See, William Barron was my uncle Billy's name. He was my mom's brother. Her maiden name was Barron. My uncle Billy died before I was born, so that's who I was named after."

"Well, why don't people just call you William?"

"Well, people do call me William. Not many do, though—pretty much just my parents, grandparents and Aunt Rose. But, you know how when you're younger you want your friends to have a nickname for you? Like, for instance, what did people call you when you were growing up?"

"Diana," she said, providing no help.

"Well, you were probably a dork," he teased. "But for the rest of us, we like a nickname. I didn't want to use Billy since that's what everyone called my uncle, so I thought it would be cool to go by Barry."

"Why not Will?"

"I wanted to be different."

"Well, Barron's different," Diana said. "You should have just had people call you Barron."

"Would you like to call me Barron?" he offered.

"No."

"Are you sure? Because I'm sensing you feel cheated for never getting to call me William, Barron, Will or Billy. I don't want there to be bad feelings later," he joked.

"I'll get over it," she assured him. And then changing the subject, she said, "Tell me about Jennifer."

"Jennifer?" Barry sighed. "Well, there's not too much to tell, really, or I guess I should say 'unfortunately,'" Barry began. "I mean, you already know about the divorce. So all that's left is, well, Jennifer. And quite frankly," Barry sighed, "she's not too interesting."

"Why'd you marry her?" Diana asked. She could feel her butt sinking into the lawn as her head continued to become one with Barry's strong and comforting shoulder. Sitting like this and listening to him talk was as soothing as hearing an old-fashioned bedtime story, the way her father used to tell them.

"I married her because I was ready. I'd moved out there to change, and after a few years, when my business was established and I started thinking about finding someone I could share my life with, I met a beautiful girl from a well-respected family, and thought, 'Why not? I'm ready to settle down. And if I can't make it work with *this* girl, I won't be able to make it work with anyone.' "

"Do you still believe that?" Diana asked.

"No. Especially not now that I know how 'beautiful' is maintained… Did my aunt tell you that Jennifer never wore sweatpants?"

"Sweatpants?" Diana had closed her eyes.

"Yeah, sweatpants. She wouldn't wear them. Not even to lay around the house in. And do you know what the reason was?"

"Hmm?"

"Sugar."

"Sugar?"

"Yeah, as in God forbid one of the neighbors should want to come over and borrow a cup of sugar when she wasn't sporting full makeup and a flattering outfit."

"I've never had to borrow a cup of sugar," Diana said, too at ease to worry if the comment made her seem big or not. After all, being in steady supply of sugar was not something she'd ordinarily boast about.

"None of the neighbors ever had to borrow any either," Barry said. "But that was her reasoning. 'What if Karen or Eric or one of the Steins should pop over for a cup of sugar? Oh no!' " The mock horror in his tone made Diana giggle. "It was like the world would end suddenly and tragically if someone rang the doorbell when her lipstick wasn't fresh or her hair had a tangle in it. You know, she actually kept a hairbrush tucked away in a drawer in every single room of the house—and I mean *every* room, laundry room not excluded."

"Are you serious?" Diana asked. She'd thought check-
ing her face in the Blue Horizon napkin dispenser had
been vain.

"Unfortunately, yes," Barry said. "The woman was constantly grooming. I mean, she couldn't even laugh without running to the nearest mirror to make sure the
movement hadn't caused any permanent damage—like,
God forbid, one of those little lines around the mouth
that prove you weren't as still as stone your entire life but
actually had occasion to smile now and then. Jennifer
lived in fear of those, too. If she went out to lunch with
a girlfriend and worried she had laughed too much for
a single afternoon, I'd catch her doing facial exercises in
front of the computer while she searched the Internet for
magical laugh-line sealant. Anyway," he continued, becoming serious, "I guess I loved her—for a while. I mean,
everyone has those little qualities that make you resist the
urge to completely cut them out of your life—even when
that urge is justified and the bad far exceeds the good.
But then it gets to the point where you realize that you
deserve more than being tied indefinitely to someone
who hurts you." Barry stopped talking and looked down
at Diana. She had fallen asleep on his shoulder. And as he
sat there holding her, in the predawn stillness of the summer night sky, he brushed one of her strawberry-blond
curls away from her face and whispered, "If only she were
the kind of girl that dreamt of azaleas, we probably would
have made it."

CHAPTER THIRTY

"Penis-butt, penis-butt, penis-butt!"

Alex Rosenfeld—the penis-butt kid. It was Diana's third day at Happy Start Nursery Camp, and already she wanted to strangle someone. The head counselor, a fifty-something-year-old woman named Bea, had told her to ignore Alex, that his incessant "penis-butt" exclamations were simply indicative of some new additions to his vocabulary and were perfectly normal for a four-year-old, so not to worry. Of course, Diana had wanted to ask why, if Alex was perfectly normal, the other kids said he had cooties and never wanted to go near him, and why, if Alex was perfectly normal, his mother's face always looked apologetic when she dropped him off and embarrassed when she picked him up, and why, if Alex was perfectly normal, he sat in the corner all day shouting "Penis-butt!" and only came up for air at lunchtime. But she didn't ask Bea any of these things. Instead, she focused on the children she did like, which was pretty much all of the rest.

Her absolute favorite child in the group was a little boy named Nicholas. Nicholas was one of those kids who seemed too cute to be real. He had big, chubby cheeks with a little nose and brown hair, and went around saying sensitive and brilliant things like, "I know my mom loves me a lot because she works two jobs, but sometimes I wish I didn't have so many toys and snacks so I could see her more." Statements like these were always coupled with curious, little-kid questions like, "Miss Diana, do you ever fart when no one's listening?" to which Diana would always smile and answer "No." So far, according to Nicholas's knowledge, Diana had never spit, pooped, fallen off the monkey bars, ate something she'd dropped on the floor, farted, flown an airplane or stolen a car.

And then there was Debra, the playground bombshell, who, despite Diana's valiant efforts *not* to be jealous of a four-year-old, constantly drove her to the greenest hills of envy. Here was a little girl with big green eyes, gorgeous auburn hair, and all the signs of perfect bone structure and a lifetime of carefree beauty. All the boys gave up their swings for her, fought with one another over whom she'd share the seesaw with, and let her cut in line at the sliding board. But Debra took it all in stride—she didn't know any different, and she probably never would. Diana was amazed by the way her skinned knees and dirty hands complemented her striking features, and wondered how the men in her *own* life would like it if *she* stopped caring about her looks and started climbing trees in an effort to capture the dramatic conflict that probably made all the boys like Debra—the fresh, natural beauty of feminine youth mingled with brazen, tomboyish playfulness.

There was only one problem: Diana wasn't four years old. If her first three days at Happy Start had taught her anything, it was that aging was unfair. Why couldn't the world be like Bea's Bumblebees—where the most important event of the day was lunch, and personal wealth was measured by how many cheese curls or chocolate cookies your mom packed you, where the biggest catastrophe was someone else playing with the yellow truck you labeled "mine," where songs were sung every hour and the ones to watch out for identified themselves by yelling "Penis-butt!" all day long. If only the world were full of Bumblebees, Diana wouldn't have lain awake the past three nights, wondering if she'd made a fool of herself in front of Barry, and hating TJ for screwing her in more ways than one.

Did Debra waste valuable cartoon time agonizing over whether Kyle really meant it when he said she'd be invited to his birthday party? Did Sally really worry that Richie was only using her as a seesaw buddy to make Debra jealous? Of course not. But then again, even if Diana could remove all conscious adult worries from her world, she'd never have a nursery camper's happy-go-lucky freedom—she'd still have to make the rent, deal with her mother, and acknowledge her knowledge of death, calories, and the fact that there was no Santa Claus. She couldn't unlearn these things.

Besides, there were still a couple of perks to not being a child: four-year-olds couldn't get drunk at bars and have mind-blowing sex. Diana guessed God had to leave *some* things for the grown-ups to enjoy (even if they occasionally led to alcoholism and disease). *God bless beer and fornication* was the only prayer she could offer when she'd watch the young smiles on the playground and know that she was stuck in the stress-filled world of adulthood for life. But then, from out of the sky—or the sliding board ladder above her head—would descend Alex Rosenfeld's endless chant, giving her faith that things weren't so bad, and that the world of adulthood could be a lot worse: she could have given birth to the penis-butt kid.

CHAPTER THIRTY-1

It was going to be a wonderful night. Candles, classical music, incredible food, and the best of company. Diana loved going to dinner at Mrs. Bartle's place. The delicious smells of whatever was cooking in the kitchen and the soothing music playing softly in the background always made her nostalgic for those "dinners at Grandma's" that she'd never really had. Diana had never known either of her grandmothers. Her father's mom had died just four months before she was born, while her mother's mom had run off to London "to find herself" the week after Mrs. Christopher, then Patty Jane Hunt, had turned fifteen. And that was why, no matter how deplorable her mother could seem at times, Diana always knew she was doing a better job than *her* mother had done; at least Mrs. Christopher had stayed in the country.

But besides the sentimental charm of home-cooked meals prepared by someone more than two generations older than her, Diana also adored and admired the elegance with which she and Mrs. Bartle dined. Her friend always laid out her best china—purchased with the first year's worth of her and Henry's savings as a first wedding anniversary gift to themselves—and they drank sparkling cider from crystal goblets, while fresh flowers and glowing candles brought sweetness and warmth to the table. And to top it all off, tonight was the Fourth of July, so if the living room curtains were open, they'd be able to catch the fireworks going off on the ball field down the street.

Mrs. Bartle had knocked on Diana's door that afternoon to invite her, explaining that it had been altogether too long since she'd cooked for her, and thrilling Diana with the words, "You look like you could use a decent meal," as she eyed her up and down with the kind of maternal suspicion that Mrs. Christopher used to display over Diana's "mysteriously" expanding waistline. It felt great to experience such skepticism in reverse. Of course, Diana had asked immediately if Barry would be joining them. After all, she had to know whether or not she should bring her mortified mask and *I-was-drunk-so-disregard-anything-stupid-I-said* sign to dinner.

"No, dear. He's back in California, tying up loose ends," Mrs. Bartle had said, her words sending an unexpected thunderbolt of disappointment Diana's way. She couldn't figure out why. Why did she feel such letdown where she'd expected to feel such relief? It felt crazy to admit even to herself, but in the strangest way, she felt betrayed. She couldn't remember everything she and Barry had talked about out on the lawn, only bits and pieces; specific words were probably lost forever. But she did remember a connection, feeling for the first time in her adult life that a man understood her, and that not all men were simple-minded and insincere—because *this* one could be her friend. But he had left so suddenly—this sweet, funny guy who still harbored guilt for taking her virginity in a one-night stand back in 1988. This guy who had undoubtedly rescued her from an endless night of self-torture and hallucinated introspection over what she could have done differently to make TJ come back for seconds. This guy who didn't think she was a freak for dreaming of azaleas and blimps and dead fathers falling from the clouds. This incredibly one-of-a-kind friend, who left without even saying goodbye.

In a way, she felt more violated by Barry's emotional hit-and-run than she did by TJ's complete lack of grown-up sexual etiquette. Maybe she shouldn't have told Barry about the azaleas. Perhaps it had scared him off. Maybe she shouldn't have slept with TJ the first night they met. But Diana had thought that was special, too. She knew what a one-night stand felt like—the back of a pickup truck, a wad of tissues, over in twelve minutes, and keeping romance out of it. It hadn't been like that with TJ. What she and TJ shared had been beautiful and gentle and sweet, and had happened in a bed, with actual sleeping involved. TJ had seen her naked, with the lights on—with her panty hose wound and stretch marks—and he'd licked his lips and smiled and, without hesitation, had gone to claim his prize, with a passion and sincerity that couldn't have been faked. It had been magical. And then, just like Barry, *poof!*—he was gone. Maybe all men were the same. Still, Diana was determined not to let some inexcusably hurtful behavior from a couple of men who weren't even in her life a month ago interfere with her enjoyment of a very special evening with a very special friend that had been the most precious part of her life for the last three years.

"Hello!" Diana called out cheerfully, as she let herself into Mrs. Bartle's apartment. Although she usually forgot to bring it with her, Mrs. Bartle had always made a point of insisting that Diana use the "emergency" key she'd been given to let herself in whenever she came to visit. Of course these insistences were always followed by assurances that never–ever–ever would Mrs. Bartle do the same with her emergency key to Diana's place. *You're like a daughter to me,* she would explain, laughing as she added, *a daughter I had when I was sixty-one years old!* And then, she'd say there was a special rule for one's children when it came to knocking at the front door: they should never have to. But as for parents and their *children's* front doors, well, the rule simply did not work in reverse.

Mrs. Bartle was in the kitchen. "Hello, dear!" she bubbled, peeking her head through the doorway. "Glad you remembered your key this time. Dinner's almost ready."

"What are we having?" Diana asked, trying to contain the excitement of her appetite. Ever since she'd started losing weight, food-related thrills made her feel like her former self—the large self that measured time by what food she was about to eat.

Mrs. Bartle put her arm around Diana's waist and, leading her into the dining room, announced proudly, "We are having eggplant parmesan with a *very* special sauce that Henry used to make, homemade pasta, hot rolls from Mario's Italian Bakery, marinated spinach, and for dessert—nothing. We're always too stuffed from dinner to want any."

Diana giggled. It was so true. "Sounds incredible, Mrs. Bartle."

"I hope you're not too warm."

"Warm?"

"My air conditioner broke. But it's supposed to be a cool night, so I thought just having the windows open would be fine." It was all right with Diana, but she didn't like the idea of Mrs. Bartle not having an air conditioner in the summer.

"Don't worry about me," Diana assured her. "But why don't I take you out tomorrow and we'll get you a new one? My treat."

"Oh, you're a sweetheart, but you save your money," Mrs. Bartle said, waving off Diana's concern. "I never turn the thing on anyway unless I have company coming over."

"Really? Don't you get hot?"

"Girlie, I don't need fancy frills like air-conditioning to make me a happy clam," Mrs. Bartle said, putting her hands on her hips. Diana laughed. Sometimes Mrs. Bartle was downright cute. "It's true! I enjoy just having the window open and getting fresh air. Besides, William will be back in town this weekend, and he'll be able to fix the dumb thing for me then."

"He will?" Diana was suddenly a bundle of nerves. How would she act in front of him? Mrs. Bartle smiled knowingly but said nothing before heading back into the kitchen, leaving Diana to wonder exactly how many stupid things she had said to Barry out on the lawn and how many of them she might be able to blame on the beer.

"So I guess you'll have someone to tuck you in again on Saturday night!" Mrs. Bartle teased from the kitchen.

"What?" Diana called back, horrified.

"You know, when you fell asleep out on the front lawn last Saturday night," Mrs. Bartle explained matter-of-factly, emerging from the kitchen with a huge bowl of pasta in her hands.

"Here, let me help you with that," Diana offered.

"It's all right, dear. I've got it," Mrs. Bartle said, setting the bowl down on the table and disappearing again into the next room. Diana's mind raced for answers—she remembered resting her head on Barry's shoulder and feeling tired, and she remembered waking up in the morning and thinking she couldn't possibly have made too big a fool of herself if she'd been sober enough to make it upstairs to her apartment, but she had no memory whatsoever of what had happened in between. What if, in her stupor, she had drooled or burped or let a snort escape when she'd laughed? What if, instead of laughing, she'd cried and allowed her nose to run right in front of him?

What if that was why he hadn't said goodbye before he left again? What if she'd grossed him out too much?

Mrs. Bartle returned to the dining room with a basket of rolls. "Let's eat!" she said excitedly, sliding into her chair.

"Everything looks so good," Diana gushed.

Mrs. Bartle looked at her sternly. "Don't change the subject."

"What subject?" Diana was merely stalling. Unfortunately, she knew her friend was nowhere near that dumb.

"Oh, come on, Diana. I'm a little old lady. How much excitement do you think I get to have?"

"Well, it's not like anything happened," Diana protested weakly, knowing that she wasn't really sure.

"Well, I know *that*."

"How?" Did Barry tell her everything?

"Because I saw you two sitting out there, and then I saw him lift you to your feet and help you stagger inside. He was back here five minutes later. I mean, I know some men are fast," she said, filling Diana's plate with food, "but no one can make up for fifteen years in *five* minutes." And there it was: Barry really *was* a nice guy, truly a gentleman. Unless, of course, he'd developed a hernia trying to lift her and was in too much pain to consider taking advantage of the situation. But Diana wouldn't allow herself to dwell on that possibility. The image of him clenching his fists not to try anything was much more appealing and a hell of a lot easier on the ego. Maybe some day she'd find out the entire truth from Barry, but for now, she'd focus on dinner with Mrs. Bartle and the one question she still had left before they could talk about anything else.

"So, were you spying on us?"

Mrs. Bartle smiled. "Like I said, Diana, how much excitement does a little old lady really get to have?"

And that was the end of the Barry conversation. For the rest of the night, the two of them simply laughed and ate and remembered what it was like to be silly. And it was a wonderful time—no self-monitoring, no playing games, no penis-butt kid, no last call, and no men; just two best friends, as close as could be, separated only by a dining room table and sixty-one years of experience, enjoying a summer evening made brilliant by the beautiful explosions of Fourth of July color that lit up the sky outside the open window.

July 5th

Dear Diary,

I was totally dreading today's weigh-in because with this brand-new schedule of sleeping at night and working during the day, I haven't managed to exercise once. I'm just too tired when I get home from the camp. The last thing in the world I can envision myself doing is getting suited up for an aerobics class with Kel. Mom was devastated, quite exaggeratedly so I might add, when I told her that despite her offer to enroll us in Kel's late afternoon class, I just didn't think I could keep up the Monday-Wednesday-Friday routine at the gym anymore. She said it was because she'd gotten so accustomed to our "together time," but I knew it was all about my weight. She's afraid I'll pork out again or something. To be honest, I *feared the same thing. That was until I kicked fear in the ass and forced myself onto the dreaded scale. I weighed 156! Could you just die? I now officially weigh less than I did when I was twenty. It's like I weigh as much as a professional female athlete who's probably a couple of inches taller than I am and is really, really muscular and stuff. But still, I think I've gotten safely out of "fat woman" range and have entered a different territory altogether. I mean, if a person hears, "She weighs 178," they've gotta think "Big girl alert!" But, "She weighs 156" just sounds more like "women's wrestling" or "pro volleyball player," or, I guess if an actual picture of my present self were to accompany the weight statement, then perhaps "voluptuous woman who could stand to lose a few pounds," but definitely not FAT, not pitifully pudgy all over, not a Queen's Closet shopper who makes do with being big because she has no choice. Look out world—I can see the size 10s now! I mean, I've still got 26 pounds to go until I am completely thin and gorgeous, but 22 pounds is an incredible start. Two more pounds and I'm halfway there! What a wonderful feeling it is to be fabulous! And speaking of fabulous, I am altogether too fabulous to get myself all upset over TJ if he doesn't show up at Scott's Tavern tonight. It'll be his loss. And if he does show up, I'm not going to sleep with him. Unless his excuse for not making any effort to see me over the last two weeks is more powerful than God (or unless I get drunk and, in that event, cannot be held accountable for the breaking of any sober and well-intended vows I've written here).*

Diana

Diana slammed the front door shut and fell to the floor in tears. She'd left the bar in a panic, and the whole way home, detained by one torturous red light after another, all she'd craved was this very moment of letting go. As she sat there, slumped over on the floor, tears clouding her vision, and shock making her tremble, the night played itself over and over, like a sickening rerun, in her mind.

TJ had been at the bar. But Diana hadn't noticed him right away. She'd actually arrived later than usual, around 11:30, so as not to seem eager or desperate or, heaven forbid, delusional. Although it really wasn't for anyone else's benefit but her own. She didn't care what the bartenders thought or what the Scott's Tavern regulars might say— she was sure they couldn't care less about her. But she wanted more for *herself* than getting there at 10:15 and waiting forever for *him* to show up. So she'd gotten there at 11:30 and, surprisingly, didn't have to wait very long before she spotted him.

He was over by the pool tables, as usual. But it was a crowded night, and Diana was on her second beer before the mass of people blocking her view had finally dispersed. And then she saw him. He looked amazing. At first, she thought she'd found a hot *new* guy to occupy her attention while she "didn't" wait for TJ. But then she realized that this hot, new guy *was* TJ, and her heart jumped into her throat. She had to tell herself: *You've slept with this man. You've seen him naked. He's seen YOU naked (eek!). There is no reason why you cannot be an adult and say hello.* And so she had stood up—knees weak, nervous chills racing throughout her body, and her mouth as dry as the kind of sand that burns the feet—and taking the deepest breath she could muster, she'd approached TJ and his friends.

"Hey, TJ," she had said, her speech feeling strangely robotic. It was a greeting so planned and so forced that the words weren't real. Now if Diana could have said what she really felt—*Hey, asshole, where the hell have you been for two weeks?*—then her hello would have been much more human. Still, it was enough to make TJ look up from his pool stick and meet Diana's gaze. But there was nothing there. No sense of a prior connection. There was no lust, no excitement, not even any awkwardness.

And all he said was, "Hey."

Her eyes wide with amazed devastation, Diana had stood there, in another new outfit from Jillie's, looking better than she'd ever seen herself look, and wondering why TJ had already gone back to playing pool. She was in the 150s now. She wasn't a big girl. She'd even started to believe she was beautiful. Why was he taking that away?

She didn't know what to do. Never when she'd play possible reunion scenarios in her head did she imagine TJ responding like this. It wasn't like she'd expected him to run to her with open arms and pick her up and twirl her around in front of his friends. But she'd expected *that* more than she'd expected this.

After the initial, punched-in-the-stomach feeling had subsided, Diana realized that she was standing amongst a group of strangers while the one person in the group who was not a stranger—the person she'd actually believed she had something with—ignored her like a hard-to-reach itch. She felt like the out-of-town guest at Cousin Dipshit's birthday party, where the only person she knew was Cousin Dipshit, who wouldn't talk to her because his *real* friends were there and he was trying to be cool. Only this time, she couldn't befriend the snack table, and there was no *I'll-tell-your-mom-on-you* threat to force TJ into decency. But if Diana had just walked away, she would have felt publicly defeated, like everybody would know that *she* knew she had failed, which could give them all something to laugh about later. Still, she felt like an even easier target just standing there. So, she chose the middle road and decided to nonchalantly slink back toward the pillar with the *Ten Reasons Why Beer Is Good For You* poster and pretend to read it before gracefully acting bored and proceeding to her seat, where she'd remain, waiting for TJ to come make it up to her. Her plan was shamefully un-Gloria-like, she knew—Steinem would stone her with feminist theory if she found out, while Gaynor would be forced to rethink the shelf life of the healing powers of "I Will Survive."

However, the Guilt Trip of the Glorias never really saw its day, for Diana's eyes were stuck somewhere around number seven on the poster—*Beer: Helping to Build Egos and Soothe Consciences for Centuries by Giving Ugly People the Confidence to Try Their Luck with the Good-Looking, and Good-Looking People Something to Blame When They Awake Next to Ugly Strangers*—when a woman with the most incredible-smelling perfume passed by and caused her to turn her head in the direction she'd vowed not to look—toward the pool tables. The woman, or girl really, wearing the perfume looked about twenty-five and possessed the exact features that Diana would have if she could totally redesign herself in any way she wanted: long, thin legs, a perfectly-rounded-yet-still-smaller-than-average butt, a tiny waist and flat stomach that, combined with a petite bone structure, made a B-cup chest look promisingly large, and those completely fatless upper arms that retain just the perfect amount of muscle, not female bodybuilder muscle, of course, but rather the kind seen on totally toned celebrity goddesses with personal trainers and heaven-sent genes. And that was just her body. She also had gorgeous, shiny, straight brown hair to her waist, exotically shaped brown eyes, a perfect nose, and a smooth and silky café au lait complexion. She had to be going with one of TJ's friends, for she stood among them,

watching the game and looking worlds more comfortable and like she belonged than Diana had when she'd
attempted the ill-fated "Hey, TJ" a couple minutes back.

There was no doubt about it—this utterly enviable
creature was definitely not the gawky outsider at Cousin
Dipshit's birthday party. Diana felt incompetent as she
watched her joke around with all the guys while TJ took
his shot. This was the kind of girl Diana had always
wanted to be—the kind that was good-looking enough,
and skinny enough, to joke freely, laugh shamelessly, and
just be herself around a group of men without worrying
if her candidness would catch her at a bad angle and give
her a double chin. Diana couldn't imagine ever being that
way. Even if she did get down to her goal weight, she'd
always be posing and planning her moves before she
made them. It made her realize what a loser she was. Even
if TJ were to fall in love with her, she'd still have this
tremendous hurdle to overcome of figuring out how to
make his friends see how charming she was in spite of
her complete incapacity to loosen up and be anything like
this girl. Maybe if Diana were more like her, TJ wouldn't
be ashamed to deliver more than a "hey" in front of his
friends.

Diana had just turned to make her move back to her
seat at the bar when a voice from the pool tables called
out, "Is that *her?*" Turning back around, she beheld the
girl she'd just been aching to become laughing sarcasti-
cally in her direction. Diana was frozen. Part of her had
wanted to run away, but another part needed to know
what this was all about. And since her feet felt like they'd

been cemented to the floor, she really had no choice but to give into the latter. So she'd turned her eyes to TJ, making contact with his for only a second before he turned to the girl, grabbed her face in his hands, and began kissing her like he'd just been reunited with the long-lost love of his life. Diana remained motionless and stunned as she watched the passionate kiss subside into a soft and starry-eyed stroking of the faces. She didn't know what was happening, but all of TJ's friends were staring at her. This was, hands down, the most humiliating event of her entire life, and all she wanted was to be home, where she could hide her face under a pillow and cry without giving anyone at Scott's the satisfaction of seeing her fall apart. And that was exactly what she was about to do when one of the guys began waving at her with exaggerated effort, like he was trying to awaken her from a trance.

"G-o h-o-m-e!" he'd called out in slow motion, treating Diana like a totally clueless imbecile who needed to be reminded of her fight-or-flight mechanism.

His words pried the couple's attention away from one another long enough for the girl to turn to Diana and hold up her left hand, on which presided a giant, square-cut diamond that sparkled like crazy even in the dimly lit bar. "Mine," she'd said, pointing to TJ, who grabbed her by the waist and lifted her off the ground. And they fell into another passionate kiss as she slithered against him to her feet.

They were *engaged?*

Diana could feel the world laughing at her as she turned to exit the bar. The room had begun to vibrate, and all background noise had harmonized into a vicious buzzing sound, quiet at first like a swarm of distant bees, but growing steadily louder as the angry bees got closer and closer to completely encircling her—to trapping her in this threatening domain of degradation and fear until she could be stung out of her misery to lie on the floor like roadkill as a reminder to all the ugly people not to substitute beer for confidence and *never* to attempt sex with people out of their league.

She had just reached the door when a light tap on her shoulder made her turn around. It was one of TJ's friends. "Listen," he'd begun. "Wait, what's your name?"

"Diana," she had said, wanting to add that it was a name far prettier than her cracking voice made it sound.

"Okay, listen, Diana," he'd said gently. "That wasn't about you. TJ and Michele have been together for five years. And every time they have a major fight, it's like a contest to see who can hurt who more. Let's just say you're not the first woman Michele has said 'mine' to. Only now that they're engaged, we all really think they're through playing games. So if I were you, I'd just leave TJ alone and forget about it. It's nothing personal. It's just the way he and Michele are."

Nothing personal? Forget about it? It wasn't personal to have all of TJ's friends staring while he and Michele made an absolute fool of her? And what about the sharp and penetrating hurt that was suffocating her more than a dozen plastic bags over the head ever could? Just forget it? Although more humane than the others, this guy was obviously a simpleton who was undoubtedly looking out for TJ's welfare, and not Diana's emotional stability, when he gave her the lamest advice known to man. But she wasn't about to stand there and challenge his logic or his motives. So she forced out a less than halfhearted "thanks" and opened the door to a world she thought she'd left behind—a world in which loneliness, defeat and self-loathing were more familiar than home.

Facing the bathroom mirror after a night of violent crying is just one more slap in the face when the body thinks it has had enough. Diana crept with caution into the truth chamber to behold exactly how much havoc her tantrum had wreaked on her face. It was a different kind of "walk of shame" than the one she was always reading about in her magazines; for, unlike the post-coital, *Aren't-I-a-naughty-girl?* strut back to one's car, apartment or dorm room, this was a totally self-inflicted shame in which it only took *one* to tango. And pink, puffy eyes and a Rudolph nose were hardly the rewards a devastated woman deserved after a night of binge crying. If only the catharsis could help accelerate weight loss or serve as a chemical peel for the face, then the hours of hysterical sobbing wouldn't seem like such an evil prank. After all, the body doesn't go through hell to actually *look* like hell—it goes through hell in hopes of looking great.

Diana lifted her eyes to the medicine cabinet mirror to discover that her hours of torment had not only failed to award her a single physical benefit, but that hell also looked worse than she remembered. A long time had passed since her last misery fest, which had been pre-pregnancy-turned-cancer-scare, pre-azaleas, pre-life-affirming-apocalypse, pre-Barry-reunion, and pre-TJ-heart-break. But if the night before had taught her anything, it was that no matter how hard she worked, and no matter how much she wanted to, she would never truly forget where she came from. For in the full spirit of her old masochistic self, Diana had suffered through a fifteen-minute car ride from the bar to her apartment, choking back all emotion and clenching her temples and teeth to prevent an accidental outburst, just so that she could savor every moment of her tearful fit—uninterrupted—in the comfort of her own home. And when she did get home, all she could do was slam the door shut and fall to the floor in a flood of endless tears and inquisition.

Why in the world had she ever thought she'd be good enough for TJ? Were her eyes going? Was she certifiable? Would she not have to be either blind or insane, or both, to think that such an Adonis would ever wish to be seen anywhere but in a dark, drunken bedroom with a woman so un-Aphrodite, a woman so unlike Michele? And what was *that* all about? The man had been in love with someone else this entire time? When he'd kissed her, when he'd licked his lips over her less-than-perfect, control-top-panty hose-inscribed body, when he'd been inside of her on the very sheets she slept on every night, when he disappeared, when he didn't show up at Scott's...that whole time he had a girlfriend that he was about to propose *marriage* to?

Why had she been such an idiot? Was she the stupidest woman on earth or was it just God's way that the moment she started feeling confident and happy it would all be taken away from her with a wave of a diamond ring? How did she become a cheap game piece in some twisted couple's sparring match? How was it that she could go from a woman who hadn't had sex in fifteen years to a woman who was viewed as discarded goods by an entire group of guys and, most likely, as a slut by the girl who had the body, hair, face, mannerisms and man that she wanted? How could she have suddenly gone from Born-Again-Virgin (although of the *by-anything-but-choice* variety) to Totally Outcast Tramp, cast into the most traumatic kind of humiliation over one, count it, ONE sexual encounter? What about the lady at the dry cleaners who had had nine? Where was her punishment? Where was her exaggeratedly more attractive competition saying "Mine"? Why wasn't the world laughing at *her?* What invisible toes had Diana stepped on to incur such devastating upset after only one little fling that had probably meant more to her than all nine of that other lady's flings put together? And why was it suddenly a "little fling"? Because that was all it had been to TJ? Or because it was over? And what was with the word "over" anyway? Was "over" not the most hopeless word in the English language? Who even invented the word "over" in the first place? Some sadistic, nihilistic bastard who thought it would be fun to cut the skimpy thread of meaning and aspiration that people like Diana believed still existed in the world? Some prick who wanted the believers to have absolutely nothing left to hold on to, nothing left to believe in, and nothing left to live for?

The only thing Diana had known for sure, as her tantrum subsided into the post-traumatic fog that would shortly be followed by sleep, was that the word "over" was definitely invented by a man, and most likely a good-looking one that, if she could travel back in time, would have been *way* out of her league. And now, now that she was awake and there were no tears left to cry, now that all was said and done with her and TJ, now that she could see the battle scars she'd given her face, she was able to understand the message in all of this: Life Sucked. It sucked for a lot of obvious reasons—she'd grown up without a father, had a mother who was a piercing pain in the ass, had known what it was like to be fat, and had had her heart plucked out and shit on by the white knight that was supposed to make all of that other stuff okay.

But at the moment, life sucked for a far less obvious reason. It sucked because in her rush to throw herself onto the floor and cry, she'd gotten out of her car without remembering to take her diary out of the glove compartment. And now that her mind was clear and her self-pity had solidified into anger, she wanted to fill those empty pages with the truth of how rotten her new bedroom buddy had turned out to be. But, of course, the thought of opening her apartment door and descending the stairs into the wretched sunlight was just too over-whelming a concept, nauseating in fact, because it would involve the risk of being seen, therefore requiring some beautification efforts on her part, and she knew she couldn't lift a hairbrush right now. However, for reasons she didn't have the energy to philosophize, being seen looking like pure hell actually seemed somewhat *less* hor-rendous than lifting a hairbrush. Besides, she had fallen asleep with her Saturday night outfit on, so she was dressed, and her hair didn't really look *that* bad. And since it was early on Sunday morning, if she went quickly, she probably wouldn't even see anyone. However, totally contrary to plan, Diana's great escape was cut short when she opened the door to find Mrs. Bartle standing outside of it with her hand raised, about to knock.

"Diana, what's wrong?" she gasped, stepping inside. "You look like hell!" The two of them stood there in si-lence while Diana tried to find a way to begin. "Do you want to talk about this, dear?" Mrs. Bartle asked gently, placing her hand on Diana's shoulder. "Because we could just sit down and *not* talk." She smiled cheerfully. "I've rented *Gentlemen Prefer Blondes.*"

"Except they don't," Diana muttered softly, thinking of the raven Michele.

"What's that, dear?" Mrs. Bartle asked, straining her neck to listen.

"He—" Diana stammered. "TJ—he's—" Her chest was heaving. She was extremely short of breath and wanted so badly not to break down and cry in front of Mrs. Bartle.

"He's what, dear? Here, come sit down." Mrs. Bartle led her to the couch.

"He's *engaged,* Mrs. Bartle!" Diana blurted, falling into hysterical sobs.

"Oh, Diana, are you sure?"

"Yes—yes—I'm sure." Diana had trouble getting the words out. Suddenly, she wanted to tell her friend everything, but every time she went to speak, she'd start gasping for air all over again. However, it only took a couple of tries for Mrs. Bartle to realize that Diana really *did* want to talk about it, and so she took the lead.

"Did you see him?" Mrs. Bartle asked. Diana nodded. "And he was with somebody else?"

"Yes," Diana choked.

"And this other girl, did he kiss her?" Diana nodded again, clenching her eyes shut in a desperate attempt to get the image out of her mind. "Was she wearing a ring?"

"YES!" Diana bawled, throwing her head forward as her shoulders shook up and down, almost violently.

Mrs. Bartle cradled her young friend in her tiny arms, *ssh*-ing and *there, there*-ing her until the wild sobs subsided into sniffles. "Diana," she began, once she knew her friend was calm enough to hear her advice, "listen to me." Lifting Diana's face to meet her own, she continued. "You did absolutely nothing wrong to deserve this. What we're dealing with here is simply a rotten apple." Diana looked at Mrs. Bartle curiously and, in spite of her anguish, couldn't help but smile a little. "Okay, so my metaphors are as old as I am," Mrs. Bartle joked, "but he's still a…a…well, Diana, let me be frank. The boy is a butt hole." Diana began to laugh, which made Mrs. Bartle laugh, too. And while they laughed, they hugged, and Mrs. Bartle helped Diana dry her tears. "Now, listen to me," Mrs. Bartle resumed seriously, cupping Diana's face in her warm and comforting hands. "Do not lose sight of everything you've worked for and all that you've gained—and you know what I mean—just because some butt hole happened to miss the boat."

Even in the midst of her heartwrenching breakdown, Diana was still blown away by her friend's intuitive wisdom. There were so many things Diana had never told her, but she knew them all. She knew that Diana had made a decision and had carried out a plan to turn her life around, a plan that had been entirely successful until now. One of Diana's biggest fears in this whole love triangle mess had been that she would slip back into her old self, and that she'd start eating incredibly decadent food again, and gain all of her weight back, and start dreaming about azaleas and blimps and anything else that could take her away from this planet. And despite her vow that she would never go backward, it had started to seem like going backward made more sense than moving forward, especially when the odds seemed to be telling her that she was a loser destined to fail at anything else she ever tried, just like she'd failed at TJ. She'd seriously begun wondering what the point was of pushing onward when more heartache was just around the corner, and had been hanging on by a string of self-respect as her only means of not giving up on the person she had created, the person she had begun to like. And here was Mrs. Bartle, her true fairy godmother if ever she had one, telling her that it was *not* okay to give up and that, more importantly, she had someone out there who realized all the work she'd done to change her life, someone who recognized where she'd succeeded, someone to help her hold on to that string—someone who'd never let her fall.

"I won't lose sight of everything I've worked for, Mrs. Bartle. I promise," Diana said. And it felt good to make that promise.

"Or all that you've gained," Mrs. Bartle reminded her.

"Or all that I've gained."

"Just because…" Mrs. Bartle hinted.

"Just because—"

"Some butt hole missed the boat!" they both finished together.

It was not the first time that Mrs. Bartle's words had given her a promise to live by.

"Swim time! Everybody go get your bags!"

Bea introduced every new activity with exclamation points. If she were an actress, the directors would constantly be reminding her to stop overacting. But Diana was never sure that Bea *was* acting. It wasn't a job requirement to seem more enthused than the children. Maybe she really *was* excited for swim time. Although, Diana couldn't see how, considering that in order to get those cute little kiddies out to the two tiny baby pools (that couldn't possibly hold all of them and, therefore, provoked many arguments) and Mr. Smiles Run-Through Sprinkler (which often broke and could only be fixed by turning off the hose and fiddling around with Mr. Smiles' head while the children grew impatient and shoved each other around to pass the time), she and Bea first had to goop up their hands with all different varieties of sun block and lather them onto the skin of each child, which was like working on a messy and smelly assembly line that talked back to you. Still, taking orders and *You're not doing it right!*s from a handful of cute little kids five days a week was a pure indulgence compared to taking orders and *You're not doing it right!*s from Mick and a horde of hungry truckers every night.

As the children scrambled to form their two sun block lines, Diana was reminded of the hilarious dance routine she'd tried at Mo's Gym on Wednesday afternoon. Mo's was different than the place she'd been going with her mother. It was fun and laid-back. And the women there weren't toothpick zombies sweating off their last ounces of body fat. They were regular women, like Diana—some chunky, some average, some thin but trying to tone up middle-age sag, all dressed in T-shirts and sweatpants or some other variation of non-threatening workout wear, none sporting spandex thongs over hot pants, and none making her feel like an oversized blueberry that didn't belong. Of course, she had to keep the whole thing a secret from her mother, who'd probably pull every muscle in her body piling on the guilt for Diana's not asking *her* to join, not that she would have. Moses J. Aaron, simply referred to as "Mo" by all who knew him, was way too progressive and improvisational for her mother. The other night, he had led them in an incredibly silly, yet exhaustingly aerobic line dance to "You Should Be Dancing" by the Bee Gees before pulling out his guitar and guiding them through a cool-down to his own rendition of Kermit the Frog's "Rainbow Connection." Mrs. Christopher just wouldn't have belonged. But Diana really felt good about herself when she was there. The two hours she'd spent at Mo's so far that week had probably been the only two hours she'd spent not nursing her heart over TJ. And in spite of the fact that everything had gone wrong where he was concerned and that six days of refusing to wallow and give up had done nothing to ease her humiliation, she was still able to rejoice in her dedication to her diet. It would have been easy to go another week without exercise and to drown each day's pain in chocolate banana muffins, cheese curls and strawberry shortcake. But then TJ and Michele would have won completely—by not only hurting and humiliating her beyond any foreseeable repair and driving her dizzy with self-analysis, but also by making her fat. And that was one satisfaction she just wouldn't give them. It was bad enough being the woman who had been publicly rejected at the bar without becoming the fat woman who let it eat her up so much that she devoured the world's food supply in some sort of twisted pie-eating contest with the rejection. If anything, the incident had given her even *more* incentive to pursue her weight loss goals. For if she were to get thin enough, like 130 pounds thin enough, she'd be too proud of her body to let her mortification over what had happened prevent her from showing it off. And if TJ were to just *happen* to see her and lose control of his pool stick in front of Michele, so be it. Thinness was the best revenge.

But payback fantasies like this would not have been enough to keep her going without the constant support of Mrs. Bartle. When she'd left Diana's apartment after the butt-hole promise on the couch, she'd told her that some people were afraid to ask for help while others *pretended* to want help when they really didn't to avoid hurting someone else's feelings. "So, Diana, do not be afraid to ask me for help—call on me every night if you need me," she had said. "But when you stop needing me, give an old fool a hint, will you?" So far, with the exception of Sunday when she'd passed out at seven o'clock, exhausted from the crying fit of the night before, there hadn't been a single night that week that Diana hadn't taken Mrs. Bartle up on her offer.

On Monday, she'd rediscovered the joy of childhood card games like War and Go Fish, which, according to Mrs. Bartle, were classic remedies for the blues. She'd had a surprisingly pleasant time but hadn't the heart or guts to admit to her friend that she saw TJ's face on every Jack and King.

On Tuesday, they'd watched *Cinderella*. Mrs. Bartle didn't think Diana was ready for flesh romance films so soon after her upset, but she did think it was important for her to realize that love was supposed to feel good, and that since she'd been feeling so terrible, TJ couldn't have possibly been her prince. Although a smart point, it was entirely lost on Diana, who was too busy wondering how it was that a man could merely dance with a woman and become obsessed with her shoe, while TJ could have SEX with a woman and *remain* obsessed with his pool stick. But afterward, she did confess to Mrs. Bartle that if she had a pair of glass slippers and a prince to put them on her feet, she'd never want to run away from herself again, no matter what cards life dealt her. So at least the movie had prompted some meaningful, non-TJ dialogue—even if it was all rooted in fairy tale wishes.

On Wednesday, operating under the theory that learning something new was truly the best way of forgetting something old—namely a problem beginning in T and ending in J—Mrs. Bartle had taught Diana how to knit. Or, more precisely, how to try. For all she'd ended up with was a sorry-looking, washcloth-size mass of misshapen yarn in place of what should have been a blanket to drape over the foot of her bed. Unfortunately, unlike cards and Cinderella, this activity had occupied enough of her mind's energy to keep her focused and obsession-free, and she'd gotten quite enthusiastic over her very first attempt at handmade décor. However, she'd been too overwhelmed with visions of how cute the little-blanket-to-be was going to look in her bedroom to notice that her novice hands had something else in mind. But Mrs. Bartle had come to her immediate rescue, insisting that it would be her greatest pleasure if Diana would let her finish the blanket over the next couple of days so that she could present it to her later as a gift. And as Diana resolved that *having* something beautiful would be more fulfilling at her hour of need than *making* something ugly, the value of art began to outweigh the value of creation, and she told Mrs. Bartle that the pleasure would be hers.

On Thursday, they'd met at Diana's place for a pajama party. Mrs. Bartle had arrived in her paisley polyester sleep set with an eager smile, triumphantly declaring, "It's Sunday night!" The words had frightened Diana at first, for she'd always considered her friend to be light-years farther away from senility than she was. But here was the constantly clearheaded sage revealing she'd drastically lost track of the days of the week. But then, Diana saw Mrs. Bartle taking ice cream, chocolate sauce, whipped cream and cherries out of the brown paper bag she'd brought—and her fear tripled. The presence of such no-no delectables could only mean one thing: she was about to get fat again. She could feel the seams of her size fourteens busting until Mrs. Bartle allowed her to deflate a little with the news that *Sundae* Night Thursday would consist of fat-free frozen yogurt, sugar-free chocolate sauce and reduced-calorie whipped cream, and that each cherry was only ten calories apiece. The 185-calorie, essentially fatless treat was so refreshing it made Diana's palate curtsey with gratitude. And to her enormous relief, she was satisfied after just one. This was the night that Diana realized the critical importance of indulging in luscious desserts even on the road to thinness. Mrs. Bartle explained that incorporating such treats into the diet was key to permanent weight loss, for the knowledge that sundaes were permitted now and then would prevent the frustrated overdosing on whole gallons of ice cream that could potentially occur if the treat were forbidden entirely. It was then and there that Diana promised that, no matter what was going on in her life, she would always honor Sundae Night Thursday and keep it holy.

★★★

"You're not doing it right!" a little voice shrieked, pulling Diana away from her reflections on how well she'd handled the week and delivering her back into camp counselor mode. She was on her third sun block customer, a chubby girl named Ellen who always insisted that the cream not be rubbed in all the way, believing that if she couldn't see it, she would get burned.

"Sorry, sweetie," Diana apologized.

"I need more!"

"You don't need more." Diana could see that Miss Bea was almost finished with her line, and she hated feeling like she was too incompetent to keep up.

"I need MORE!" Ellen continued to protest, crossing her arms in front of her chest and refusing to move out of the way. Diana could feel Miss Bea watching her. She needed to remain patient.

"All right, Ellen, one more little squirt," she conceded, dabbing a bit more sun block onto the pesky brat's right arm and guiding her out of the line.

"You're NOT doing it right!" Ellen whined, resisting Diana's efforts to move her. "You need to put more on my other arm, too!"

"Fine," Diana snapped, resentfully obeying the request.

"Hey, Miss Diana," the next child said as Ellen finally left the line. It was Randy, a guilty-looking little boy who had never been officially charged with committing any actual crimes but, nevertheless, had a creepy demeanor about him, like he'd always just finished killing someone.

"Yes, Randy?" she asked, opening his bottle of sun block.

Randy smiled mischievously, as if he was about to confess to some hideous deed and laugh wickedly at her terror. "Your butt is fat."

Diana could hear the other children giggling, even Nicholas, her favorite. She wanted to crawl out of camp—backward, so no one could make fun of the view—and fall asleep under a parked car. Children were supposed to be kinder than the rest of the world. They were supposed to be innocent and untainted by the body-obsessed mania of popular culture. They weren't supposed to know a nice ass from a fat one, and if they did, they weren't supposed to broadcast it and make the ass's bearer want to go hibernate under a Toyota. She didn't have a clue as to how to handle this, at least not a clue that didn't involve reaching out her hands and clawing Randy's face off or fleeing the scene and disappearing off the face of the universe, or both. Maybe she could reverse the situation, and become the last *laugher* instead of the last *laughee*, by cracking some witty insult against Randy that the children would understand but that wouldn't get her fired.

"Hey, Randy," she began, her head spinning with the lack of available possibilities with which she could complete the statement. "Um…"

"Hey, Miss Diana!" called Jodi, the little girl at the back of the line that never went anywhere without her sidekick, Beanie, a doll whose naked rear end, exposed by the simple pull of a Velcro flap, was a constant source of amusement for the other children.

"Yes? What is it, Jodi?" Diana asked sweetly. Translation:

Please, please, please say something—anything—to make these mini demons stop laughing at me!

"Miss Diana Fat Butt!" Jodi sang out, swinging a bare-assed Beanie in the air as she beamed at her clever use of words.

"That's not nice, Jodi," Bea reprimanded. "You and Randy should tell Miss Diana that you're sorry. Remember what I told all of you about Bea's Bumblebees?"

"We don't sting!" the campers shouted in unison, like robots.

"That's right!" Bea chirped proudly. "We're nice bees. And what do nice bees say when they've hurt somebody's feelings?"

"Sorry!" the chorus replied, with absolutely no sincerity whatsoever.

"That's right!" Bea gushed again, as if the realization that her Bumblebees weren't total imbeciles, and could actually answer questions they'd already been fed the answers to, were enough to give her an orgasm. But even worse than this overdone display of enthusiasm was the fact that now Diana was not just the camp counselor with the fat butt that the children had laughed at, but the camp counselor with the fat butt that had to be *rescued* from their ridicule by a frighteningly cheerful wackadoodle whose idea of humor was attempting bad puns on her own name. "Diana," Bea said quietly, leaning over for a little counselor's conference, "I'm about to buzz off to the little bee's room. Could you watch the children until I get back and then we'll go outside?" Diana nodded, wondering why in the world the woman insisted on maintaining the corny lingo when the children weren't even listening.

As soon as Bea was gone, Alex Rosenfeld shifted into penis–butt gear.

"Penis–butt! Penis–butt!"

"Miss Diana?" Nicholas said shyly as he handed her his sun block.

"Yes?" Diana asked, watching smug, malicious Randy trot off to the toy box and wishing she hadn't had any part in protecting his skin from the harmful rays of the sun.

"Penis–butt! Penis–butt!"

"I don't think your butt is fat," Nicholas said apologetically.

"Penis–butt! Penis–butt!"

"Thank you, Nicholas," Diana said, smiling gratefully at this one saving grace in the demeaning plight of her big-ass existence.

"Penis–butt! Penis–butt!"

"Hey, Miss Diana," Randy said, running up to her from behind with a plastic yellow truck. "You don't have a fat butt… You have a fat butt-*head!*" He laughed, moving his face closer to hers the way little kids do when trying to command adult attention.

"Penis–butt-HEAD!" Alex suddenly called out, causing everyone to turn and stare at him in amazement over the variation.

"That's not funny, Randy," Diana reproached, no longer concerned with preserving her popularity and not letting the children see her sweat.

"*You're* not funny," he smart-alecked back to her as

she finished with Nicholas and began lathering up her last in line.

"Penis-butt-head! Penis-butt-head!"

"Don't talk to me like that, Randy," Diana warned nervously. She wasn't used to standing up for herself, not even to four-year-old brats. And as much as she knew that she was letting Randy intimidate her by not looking him in the eye when she was chiding him, she found it tremendously hard to make that kind of contact, like if she did, he'd be able to see—and laugh at—the world of insecurity she was trying to conceal in her supposed concentration on SPF 40-ing Jodi's fair arms.

"Yeah, don't talk to her like that, *Randy,*" a boy named Felix chimed in.

"Penis-butt-head! Penis-butt-head!"

"Shut up, *Felix!* You were named after a *cat,*" Randy taunted.

"Both of you, cool it," Diana said, finishing up with Jodi's sun block and rising to her feet.

"I see Miss Diana's fat butt!" Randy teased, falling into a fit of convulsive laughter that gave him an excuse to bump into Felix, who fell immediately to the ground. Felix then pushed Randy, who pulled Felix's hair, at which final straw, Felix pinched Randy's leg until he fell to the ground as well.

"Penis-butt-head! Penis-butt-head!" And *that* was really getting annoying.

"Alex! Please stop saying that!" she begged, raising her voice a little as she bent down to break Felix and Randy apart.

"Penis-butt-head! Penis-butt-head!"

Felix had started to cry, giving Randy even more fuel for combat. "Crybaby! Crybaby! Felix is a crybaby!" he shouted, hiding behind Diana and grabbing on to each of her outer thighs as he poked his head in and out of Felix's view in a *Now-you-see-me, now-you-don't (because-I'm-hiding-behind-a-great-fat-ass)* kind of way.

Felix ran over to Diana and buried his face in her stomach. "Miss Diana, make him stop!" he pleaded.

"Randy, stop that," Diana said, turning around to the devil on her back, who suddenly swung himself around to the front of her, knocking Felix to the floor once again.

"Penis-butt-head! Penis-butt-head!"

"Randy, you apologize to Felix right now!" she yelled, too frustrated to realize it was probably the first time she'd ever actually yelled at anyone.

"Penis-butt-head! Penis-butt-head!"

"He started it!" Randy protested.

The other children had grown restless waiting to go swimming and had begun to run around the room, bumping into chairs and each other—with the exception of Alex, of course, who stood still amidst the disorder and continued his mantra, uninterrupted.

"Penis-butt-head! Penis-butt-head!"

Diana bent over to help Felix to his feet.

"Penis-butt-head! Penis-butt-head!"

"Alex, quiet!" she shouted. Normally, she could tolerate this bizarre child's "harmless" chant, but at this moment, it simply quadrupled the chaos. Felix, done crying now, must have taken a swing at Randy while Diana was looking at Alex, for the loud clapping sound that turned her attention back in their direction was followed by Randy crying and grabbing his own face as he kicked violently at Felix's shin.

"Penis-butt-head! Penis-butt-head!"

"Now, Randy, what is going on?" Diana demanded.

"Penis-butt-head! Penis-butt-head!"

"He hit me!" Randy whined, reaching down to slug Felix, who was seated on the floor, holding his distressed leg. But Diana grabbed his arm mid-swing. "Let go of me!" he yelled, wriggling his little arm around in her grip.

"Penis-butt-head! Penis-butt-head!"

"I'll let go of you if you apologize to Felix and promise to go sit in the corner until Miss Bea gets back."

"Penis-butt-head! Penis-butt-head!"

"No!" Randy shouted. "I'm not sorry! I hate him! Let go of me!"

"Penis-butt-head! Penis-butt-head!"

"No, Randy. First tell Felix you're sorry." Diana really didn't know how to handle this, fearing that the second she let go of Randy, he would attack Felix.

"Penis-butt-head! Penis-butt-head!"

Suddenly, there was a bang. And a loud wailing sound erupted from the other side of the room. Diana turned to see who the victim was, loosening her grip on Randy's arm. It was Debra—beautiful, Miss Toddler America Debra. She had fallen into an easel, which now lay entangled with her on the floor. This was beginning to feel like a bad dream.

"Penis-butt-head! Penis-butt-head!" And she really

wanted Alex to go bury his face in the soil of some other continent where she wouldn't have to hear that ridiculously irritating chant for the rest of her days.

"I hate you!" Randy yelled, sinking his teeth into Diana's hand and setting his arm free. His bite stung like a thousand bees and everything became blurry for a few moments. She wanted to hurt him—the little shit had broken the skin and her hand was actually bleeding. But she couldn't even go take care of herself until Bea got back.

"That's it, Randy!" Diana threatened. Although, she wasn't exactly sure what she threatened him with. How could she threaten a demonic four-year-old who obviously feared nothing?

"Penis-butt-head! Penis-butt-head!"

Debra continued to cry in the background. Diana knew she needed to go to her.

"Fat butt! Fat butt!" Randy taunted, laughing, as Diana turned to help Debra.

"Randy!" she yelled, spiraling back around. She had finally lost her temper.

"Penis-butt-head! Penis-butt-head!"

Debra's cry was now a high-pitched moan, haunting in its desperation.

"Penis-butt-head! Penis-butt-head!"

"Alex! Please!" Diana shouted. She knew she had lost control. Her biggest concern was Debra, but she just couldn't seem to make it over there amongst all the distractions.

"Penis-butt-head! Penis-butt-head!"

And then, suddenly, she snapped. "OH, WOULD YOU

JUST SHUT YOUR BIG, FAT MOUTH, YOU LIT-TLE FREAK?"

As soon as she'd said the words, she couldn't believe they had actually sprung from her own mouth. The entire room was silent. Debra had stopped crying. The children had stopped clamoring. And Randy and Felix had stopped fighting. Bea had even gotten back from the bathroom just in time to hear Diana's outburst, and she stood in the doorway, gaping at her like she'd just pulled a gun on the poor boy. The silence blared for a miniature eternity until it was finally replaced by a sound worlds more awful. It was the slow and steadily rising howl of a little boy who had just been scarred for life in front of his playgroup. Alex Rosenfeld's perverse incantation had finally worn itself out, only to be replaced by a sound that would be even harder to get out of the head. For he cried as violently and gasped as desperately as if he'd just seen his entire family ripped to shreds by wolves. It was a noise that would burn forever in Diana's brain, and she felt horrible. All she could do was stand there, frozen, waiting for the cops to arrest her for verbal violence.

"I think you ought to go see Arlene," Bea said softly, with a look of frighteningly uncharacteristic sternness, as she put her arms around Alex and attempted to comfort him.

Arlene was Happy Start's camp director and nursery school principal, the one who had interviewed Diana for the job, the one who had hired her, and, undoubtedly, the one who would now fire her. As Diana walked out of the room, she saw Nicholas staring at her with heartbreak-

ingly innocent eyes, and she realized that he, and all of
the other children, would forever remember her as a
monstrous villain that had revealed her true identity when
she'd exploded on the strange kid in front of the entire
room, teaching them all that it wasn't okay to be different. It was at that moment that she decided to skip the
stop into Arlene's office—she knew she was never coming back. And so she simply went straight to her car, with
intentions to drive it as far away from Happy Start as she
could get on a quarter tank of gas. But once she was inside its doors, and sheltered from the eyes and cries of the
children, Diana realized that it wasn't how far she could
escape *physically* that was important, but rather how far
she could remove her mind from dwelling on something
she knew she could never change. And since she only
knew of one remedy for escaping her own mind, she
headed straight for the bar, leaving Happy Start behind
forever as she traveled on toward what she hoped would
at least be a Happy Hour.

Figuring she'd be safe from TJ and his friends on a Friday before sunset, Diana had come to Scott's to try her
hand at hard liquor, which she'd decided would be the
best way to dull her shock. She had just sampled her first-
ever whisky sour, which tasted like a sweat sock soaked
in arsenic and, therefore, had to be ingested in extremely
spaced-out baby sips. Still, she felt sophisticated sipping
cocktails in the broad daylight with a bunch of businessy
types at the end of a tough workweek. It was completely
different from the sexually charged, beer-guzzling atmo-

sphere of a Saturday night. Hopefully, the relaxed, TJ-free environment would really enable her to concentrate on cultivating a nice buzz, which, at the rate she was nursing her whisky sour, might take a while. But she had no place to be. She'd already decided to skip Mo's for one afternoon and had even called Mrs. Bartle to say she wouldn't be around that night for her usual help session.

"Is that a hint?" Mrs. Bartle had joked, reminding Diana of her request to be clued in when her support services were no longer necessary. Diana didn't have the heart to tell her friend that, unfortunately, it wasn't a hint at all, that despite the card games, fairy tale, knitting lesson and low-calorie sundae, she was still in as much, if not more, trouble, for just when she believed she could still handle life, even with a broken heart, she had managed to screw hers up even further. And she'd screwed it up by doing something that even Mrs. Bartle wouldn't be able to find sympathy for. How could Diana make her empathize with being fired because she'd been so brutally honest to a child that she'd made him cry? It was one thing to make Diana feel justified in being heartbroken, but how would this sweet and gentle woman—this woman who'd probably never hurt anyone's feelings in her entire life—possibly rationalize her calling a four-year-old boy a freak in front of a roomful of children, especially when all of these children, except for the freak in question, already knew? This was definitely something she'd have to handle on her own, without running to Mrs. Bartle for comfort.

Still, she would definitely need her tomorrow night,

for it would be her first Scott's-free Saturday night since adopting her new lease on life. She hadn't spent a single Saturday night at home since before the tumor blimp, but at this point, she needed to make herself scarce for a while. Her plan was to wait twenty-six pounds before allowing TJ to see her again, at which time she would refuse to give him the time of day—even if he begged for it. She ended up answering "maybe" to Mrs. Bartle's *Is-that-a-hint-that-you-no-longer-need-me* question, figuring that it was as close to the truth as she could get without revealing what had just happened and how she actually planned to deal with it—which was by getting so drunk that she'd be able to wander home in a fog and fall fast asleep without thinking about the unemployed mess she'd just made of her life. Mrs. Bartle had seemed to understand the "maybe," following it with a "Perhaps I'll see you tomorrow night, then" and a few sentences about Barry coming into town and the three of them possibly having dinner.

"Tell him to fix your air conditioner, and I'll be there," Diana had joked, unsure of how sincere her attempt at lightheartedness sounded and of how she would feel facing Barry as a woman who not only dreamt of azaleas, tumor blimps and fathers resurrecting out of the clouds, but also abused children in real life.

She didn't get it. She had always prided herself on being great with kids. Even when she was 178 pounds and working at Blue Horizon without having had sex in fifteen years, one of the very few positive truths with which she could credit herself was that she would make an incredible mom some day. How in the world could she say that now? Why had she allowed herself to lose it like that with Alex? *Penis-butt-head! Penis-butt-head!* So what? He was only four. If only Randy hadn't antagonized her like that; if only he hadn't made her so aggressive. But she really didn't harbor any guilt where he was concerned. If anything, she thought she had been too tolerant with Randy. Then again, what was *normal?* How would a normal person, who didn't make such tremendous mistakes, have handled a child attacking another child and then biting the hand that restrained him? Maybe she wasn't supposed to know the answer. Maybe her explosion in front of the kids and her permanent leave of absence from Happy Start was God's way of sparing her from obsessing over the "fat butt" comments that had ignited the whole disaster. For although Diana never thought that matters of her weight could ever seem trivial—not even when she believed she was at death's door—trivial is exactly what worrying about the motivating factors and ultimate truth value in Randy's original "fat butt" remark seemed now. Perhaps in fighting with four-year-olds and flipping out on socially underdeveloped outcasts, she had matured.

"I'll take a vodka tonic," a female voice spoke over her shoulder. Vodka tonic. Diana would have to remember that for her next one. It had a classy ring to it, and anything had to taste better than what she was drinking now. "Well, look who it is!" The saccharine-coated tone made Diana turn around, and staring her in the face were a pair of beautiful and exotic dark brown eyes belonging to a face she would never forget. It was Michele. "How *are* you?" she squealed with exaggerated, cheerleader enthusiasm. Her hair was wrapped up in a thick bun, and she was wearing one of those tailored, career-woman suits, the kind with the short skirts that always look so much sexier on actresses portraying executives than they do on real women who actually *are* executives. But of course, Michele bore a striking resemblance to the pretend variety. Next to her, Diana, dressed in a pair of khaki shorts, a T-shirt and sneakers, suddenly felt like the farm girl who moved to Beverly Hills from the sticks and wore a hand-me-down church dress to the prom. Her outfit was poor and boring, just like she was. "Diane, right?" Michele continued, overly friendly.

"Diana." She wished Michele would just get to the point and tell her off already, but at the same time, she was completely mesmerized by her and wanted not only to memorize what made her so gorgeous so that she could attempt to copy it, but also to be seen associating with a woman who, in high school, would have been the girl that everybody worshiped. Diana had a feeling such was true in Michele's post-graduate life as well, for even though she felt this vixen was about to tear her to shreds, she couldn't help but feel it was her place to sit there and take it, for to do otherwise would be overstepping her bounds where such superiority was concerned.

"Diana," Michele corrected herself, flashing the whitest smile the world had ever seen as she ushered forth the two women standing behind her. "I'd like you to meet my two best friends, Stephanie and Holly."

"Hi," Diana said quietly, briefly considering that, per-haps, Michele was being nice for real, but quickly com-ing to her senses—and realizing her naive capacity for underestimating the cruelty of others—when she saw the daggers shooting out of these women's eyes. Both were dressed exactly like Michele, just in different col-ors, but neither looked nearly as good. All three of them seemed as if they worked somewhere important, like at an advertising agency or one of those mysterious corpo-rations from a nighttime soap opera, the kind that sup-posedly control all the big business in the state but never actually specify what it is they do.

"Stephanie and Holly are going to be bridesmaids at my wedding," Michele said. Diana stared at her blankly. She suddenly knew exactly where this was going, and she didn't have the energy to come up with the words to pre-tend she didn't. "You know, my *wedding* on the 21st of October…when I marry TJ." Michele batted her eye-lashes at the sound of his name, as if Diana wouldn't have understood whom she meant without the emphasis. Ei-ther Stephanie or Holly, depending on which was which, had walked around to the other side of Diana's chair, lean-ing her elbows on the bar so that their shoulders were practically touching, while the other bridesmaid-to-be stood by Michele, glaring at Diana like she could actu-ally *hear* her wondering how awful it must be to live in the shadow of someone so much better looking without ever having a mind of one's own. "Oh, silly me!" Michele laughed, taking a sip of her drink. "I forgot to mention," she began, looking from one friend to the other, and then straight into Diana's eyes, "Diana is the *whore* who slept with my fiancé."

Diana had been hurt many times in her life, and by many people. She'd heard "fat ass" behind her back a million times from strangers—mainly impatient customers at the diner and sexually frustrated teenage boys yelling out of car windows—and she'd imagined far worse things coming from the mouths of people who actually *knew* her when she wasn't around to hear them, but never had any words, real or imagined, burned as bitterly as these. Never had anyone looked her directly in the face and said something to make her feel as dirty, immoral, and disgusting as Michele just had. She could feel the water springing to her eyes.

"Aw," Michele cooed, maliciously sarcastic. "Are we going to cry?" Despite Diana's efforts at restraint, the tears began to stream down her face faster than she could wipe them away. "Oh, you poor thing! Stephanie, Holly, look! She cries *real* tears!" she exclaimed, like a little girl in a doll commercial. "She drinks, she blinks, she sleeps with other people's fiancés, she *definitely* eats...ah," Michele sighed, as if overwhelmed by awe. "And she even cries!"

"Mommy! Mommy! Can I take her home?" chirped the clone next to Michele, and they all laughed.

"But he wasn't your fiancé when I...when..." Diana fumbled for the right words. She had never been so afraid to speak in her entire life, but she felt like she had no choice. If she got up to leave, they'd probably just beat her into staying for more torment. And no one would even try to stop them because Michele was so beautiful. "You guys were broken up… I didn't even know—"

"Shut up!" Michele interrupted loudly, moving her face even closer to Diana's. "Shut up. Don't you tell me what we *were* or what you *knew*. You don't know a fuck-ing thing about TJ and me. And neither one of us gives a *damn* about you or what you *think* you knew. You don't know shit," she finished, pulling away again. It was in this moment, as Michele retreated back into her own space, that Diana suddenly remembered what TJ's friend had told her—that she hadn't been the first woman that Michele had said "mine" to—and, out of nowhere, even though she was crying, and even though she felt terri-fied, she found the voice to challenge her.

"Do you treat *all* the women your fiancé sleeps with this way? Or just the ones you feel threatened by?" She couldn't believe she'd said it, but the look on Michele's face made it worth the risk. She looked like she'd just *walked in* on TJ and Diana having sex, like maybe she was about to go cry herself. But after a little while, her ex-pression began to change, slowly revealing the harshest resentment Diana had ever seen. It was an expression she had trouble believing she'd caused, an expression she was still in the midst of being intrigued by when Michele sud-denly reached out and slapped her clear across the jaw-line. It was a smack heard throughout the entire bar, and there wasn't a single head in the room that didn't turn to see where it had come from.

The bartender rushed over to them. "Is everything okay here, ladies?" Michele had not yet taken her eyes off of Diana, and Stephanie and Holly were now both at her side, each of them holding on to her and telling her it would be all right. Even in her numbness, Diana still recognized the criminally unfair irony of the fact that if TJ were there, he'd be leading Michele's comfort pack. "Well, if none of you are gonna answer me, I'm gonna have to ask all of you to leave," the bartender continued.

"I'll go," Diana volunteered, reaching into her pocket and leaving a couple of dollars on the bar. Her face was throbbing as she stood up and began walking away, and, although the shock had stopped her tears, she was trembling and knew she had to get out into the open air before she fainted.

"Here, keep it!" Michele called out from behind her, shoving the money against Diana's back and letting it fall to the floor. "TJ says two dollars is all you're worth!" But Diana just took a deep breath and kept right on going.

"Now, you behave yourself, little girl, or you're out, too," she heard the bartender say jokingly. It was almost flirtatious. How was it that Michele had openly assaulted her but was able to stick around for what would probably be a few drinks on the house to make her pretty face smile again, while Diana was the one leaving with her tail between her legs like a piece of trash? She could feel every Happy Hour eye staring at her, half in pity and half in relief that it wasn't them taking that shameful, beaten down walk to the door. It was her largest public defeat to date. And it would be her last. For she was never going to leave her apartment building again.

The tears returned once she was safe from view, but

the air outside was so unmercifully hot that it wasn't any easier to breathe. Maybe she didn't deserve to. Maybe she'd been a fool all along for thinking she had changed for the better. What was better about her life now? Only one thing: she was thinner. Big deal. She'd still been called fat twice in one day, once by a four-year-old demon-creep and once by the almighty Michele whose "She *definitely* eats" definitely counted as "You're fat." At least when she weighed 178, she'd never been fired or slugged in the face. She was ready to give up. Whatever "giving up" meant. What was left to give? She'd already lost so much—her job, TJ, her dignity. All she had left to forfeit was weighing less. But at the moment, the idea of finding food to binge on so that she could finish herself off just seemed nauseating, not to mention exhausting.

She didn't even wait for the air-conditioning in her car to take effect before speeding off toward home. The thick, stuffy heat in there made the thick, stuffy heat outside seem like a walk-in-freezer, but enduring it was preferable to waiting in the parking lot where, at any moment, Michele and her entourage could come out and liquidate her. She didn't really want to go home, but home was the only spot she knew she could hide. She wasn't about to be seen in another public place, not even a convenience store, looking the way that she felt.

It was beyond comprehension that she'd gone through an entire childhood and adolescence without ever once being hit only to be smacked across the face so hard it echoed at age thirty-two in a bar—and during Happy Hour, no less, which hardly seemed like a natural brawl time. It was the kind of thing that made her want to run to Mommy and sob her guts out while telling the story of how the barroom bully attacked her. That is, if "Mommy" weren't her *own* mother, who hadn't been present for a sob story since Diana was four and a neighbor's dog chased her down a hill and made her fall and rip her stockings. And even then, her mother had made her feel like she deserved it by saying that Russell the Saint Bernard was the sweetest dog on the block and had only wanted to play with her, and that those were very expensive stockings she'd ripped, and now she'd have nothing to cover her legs with when she wore her turquoise-and-navy dress, for only "loose" women wore dresses without hosiery, and the younger she learned that the better, so perhaps her run-in with Russell had been a blessing in disguise, for it had given her a lesson on class. If her mother couldn't make her feel better then, there was no way she'd be able to make her feel better now.

The only person, besides her father, that could ever make her feel better lived in the direction of home anyway. Mrs. Bartle had made her see the light so many times before. Maybe she could help Diana glue her life back together again this one last time. For after this, it was no more mistakes. No more delusions that she could be something she was not. No more goals. No more crushes. No more fantasies. The only thing she would try to keep up with was losing weight, but not because she wanted to attract some guy who would just end up hurting her and not because she harbored any secret wishes of becoming one of the world's Micheles. She'd do it because the thinner one becomes, the less of a target she is. Hell, she could've obliterated the entire scene at Happy Start that had rendered her essentially fired *and* reduced at least a fraction of Michele's insults by weighing 130 or less. Less was always better.

She would definitely resume classes at Mo's next week. Maybe she'd even become anorexic or bulimic for a little while. Diana tried to imagine herself being discovered facedown in a pool of blood on the bathroom floor— her size eights hanging loosely around her jutting hip bones—and being rushed to the hospital where her mother would be beside herself with guilt and *Why? Why?*'s as she looked on in horror at what her years of criticism and locking the refrigerator doors had done to her only child. This was one fantasy Diana would allow, however, because illusions of self-destruction could only make her real life seem better. And they were truly harmless illusions, for even though she had no will to keep going, her will to die or severely screw up her health was even weaker. She didn't have the strength to be suicidal.

An ambulance forced Diana to the side of the road as she turned onto Elizabeth Court. She watched its swirling lights disappear behind the giant maples that lined the street, and as the sound of the siren grew fainter in the distance, she realized that if she ever *were* to do anything to herself, as model-thin as it might make her, it would be that sound—the sound of speeding sirens—that would deliver her to the glorious reception of guilt and apologies she'd envisioned from her mother. Not a very glamorous way to hitch a ride to *I'm sorry.* Besides, what if her *mother-come-find-me* fantasy didn't go according to plan and poor old Mrs. Bartle were the one to find her on the bathroom floor in a size-eight pool of blood instead? What then? Yes, her mother would be sorry, but probably not as sorry as if she had found her herself, and Mrs. Bartle—sweet, loving, makes-everything-okay Mrs. Bartle—would be the one forever stuck with the horrifying visual that was really intended for Mommy. And that would just be all wrong. Just the inkling of possibility—as minuscule as it was, for her death wish days had pretty much flown away on the tumor blimp—made her feel guilty.

Diana knew Mrs. Bartle would be hurt beyond comprehension if she were to ever deliberately harm herself. And, although it was an emotion Diana had never seen in her, she also had a feeling that her friend would be angry—and with more than just cause. For it was always Mrs. Bartle who had provided her with the encouragement to have courage in the face of all things adversarial, the insight to understand what had passed, and the foresight to see tomorrow. How could she even consider devaluing the wealth that woman had given her by fantasizing about throwing it all away?

Diana pulled away from the curb. As she proceeded down the road, she pictured herself telling her best friend everything about her day, including not just her own *feel-sorry-for-me* collapse into victimhood but also her brief, but life-altering stint at victimization, not just the part that would summon a friendly, *cry-on-me* shoulder, but also the part that might warrant a cold one. She was no longer worried about the potential harshness of her friend's response to what she had done to the little boy who cried penis-butt. If Mrs. Bartle were going to be unsympathetic, she'd be unsympathetic for a very good reason. And if she were going to be understanding, then perhaps she'd prove that Diana had been too hard on herself. Either way, she would be honest. Diana could always count on her for that. And through her honesty, Diana would finally gain some perspective on the chain of events that had spiraled so out of control, she'd turned into an unemployed monster that fought in bars. Maybe Mrs. Bartle would tell her that's exactly what she was—a monster. Maybe she'd say the smack that woke the world was exactly what Diana deserved and that it probably hurt her far less than she'd hurt the poor, little four-year-old she'd bruised irreparably with her words. But it didn't seem very likely that Mrs. Bartle would say either. And those being the worst imaginable ramifications of her telling her friend the entire truth about her bad day, she knew it wouldn't be such a rotten, miserable night—or such a rotten, miserable *life*—after all. All she needed to do was go home and tell Mrs. Bartle everything that had happened, and then everything would be okay.

Red flashes of dizzying light bounced off of her sun-soaked windshield as she turned onto Starry Lane and drove past the flaming marigold island that housed the Glen Vali Suites sign. The ambulance, the one that had passed her on Elizabeth Court, had come here—to her apartment complex.

Seeing an ambulance parked outside of a building,

without its siren blaring, was always more disturbing to Diana than seeing the ones that sped deafeningly past traffic on the street. It becomes more real, more permanent, when the "where" is known, that crucial component of the who-what-where trinity that governs curious rubberneckers, concerned citizens, and anyone with a human pulse during times of tragedy. Diana pulled into her parking spot and said a silent prayer for Louie Spaghetti.

Louie was the nice-as-could-be embodiment of jolly obesity that lived in the building next to hers. He reminded everyone of an Italian Santa Claus, so, naturally, all the tenants adored him. His real last name began with an "S" and was, perhaps, too complicated for even him to pronounce, for he introduced himself to everyone he met as "You can just call me Louie Spaghetti." Diana had heard it said, out of what some might call neighborly concern, but she preferred to think of as ignorant fat-bashing, that Louie was a walking heart attack. He'd had three close calls in the past year and a half, but they'd all been false alarms. Still, an ambulance at Glen Vali Suites generally meant that Louie Spaghetti was in trouble.

Staring with pity at Building B, Diana realized how downright stupid she'd been for letting some dumb kids and a mental prima donna make her envision her own blood as a pool for drowning in. It was the first time she'd truly understood the absurdity of letting other people dictate whether or not she had a right to enjoy her life and live it without self-loathing and self-destructive scenarios giving encore performances in her head. Allowing herself to get caught up in these *I-am-*

a-public-failure-who-must-be-punished modes was neither fashionably masochistic—like five-foot-ten-inch runway models starving themselves below the 120s to fit a prototype—nor was it the slightest bit permissible, even in light of her recent devastations. Thinking of Louie Spaghetti and the possibility that, unlike his three lucky strike-outs, this might be the real hit, made Diana feel like the biggest jerk on earth—for not only taking her own health for granted, but for seeing it as expendable, like it was a piece of sacrificial trash that could be thrown away to make her mother and the likes of TJ and Michele pity her.

Crossing her fingers for Louie as she bit anxiously on her bottom lip, Diana got out of the car. But as she neared the entrance to her apartment, she realized that it couldn't be Louie Spaghetti that was in trouble, for it was the doors of her *own* building that had been propped open by the paramedics. Although at first a little relieved, a fear was growing in the pit of Diana's stomach—which one of her neighbors was in trouble? Was it someone she'd passed a million times on the stairs? Someone she'd held the door for? Someone she could have been nicer to? She needed to go get the scoop from Mrs. Bartle who, for a little old lady that kept out of other people's business, sure seemed to know what was going on before everybody else usually did. Diana attempted to squeeze past the paramedics, but the man in the doorway stopped her.

"Excuse me, ma'am. We've got medical personnel coming through. If you would just step aside, please."

"Sure," Diana complied softly, noticing that a small crowd had assembled around the ambulance. Feeling typically antisocial, but nevertheless unsure of where to go, she found herself drifting into the gathering of rubberneckers, concerned citizens and human hearts that waited beneath the revolving light for answers.

"Yeah, I heard she called 911 but was dead before they could ask for her emergency," said one man that Diana only vaguely recognized. The others hardly looked familiar at all. She wondered if any of them knew who *she* was, and pretty much hoped that they didn't. For although not being recognized would prove an undeniable testament to her unfortunate lack of popularity, she'd rather be unpopular than identified and, heaven forbid, spoken to. She was in no mood.

"She was such a nice lady," said another man, who was supported by a light chorus of agreement.

"Never bothered a single soul," one woman reflected sadly, sighing into the crowd.

"Now, who was it again?" asked a twenty-something girl, squinting at the doors as the paramedics emerged carrying a stretcher. The sheet was pulled all the way up, covering the face of whoever lay on top of it.

"It was that old lady," the first man answered. "Down in room 101. Bartle. Everyone just called her Mrs. Bartle. They say it was a heat stroke."

A skin-numbing chill spread over Diana's arms and legs, gripping them violently and threatening to shatter her bones. She couldn't see anything but the bleeding red light swimming around on the blinding white sheet that hid the body. Words whirred around her like broken sounds. And people were just blotches of dull color, with nothing fitting together to make any kind of sense, like random streaks on the canvas of the most poorly attempted impressionist painting the world had ever seen. A blob of flesh reached out toward her face. It was probably a hand. Or an arm of some sort—or someone—a person, a dull blotch of senseless color, wanting to help. But Diana couldn't be helped, not by this free-floating mass trying to grab at her. And so she swung at it. But she only hit air. Hot, steamy, cold, clammy, mean, malicious, murderous, unforgiving air. And she ran.

She ran either very fast or very slow, depending on the speed of the broken sounds and blotchy streaks around her, which she was unsure of. But she knew that at whatever pace the world was going, she was going opposite. And after a minute, second, hour or year, she smashed into a metal box that seemed to crack every bone in her ribs. But she only knew this because she heard the collision and the suffering cry from within. She couldn't feel a single thing.

The jingle jangles in her hand let her inside of the box, turning it into a warm and familiar furnace where she could scream. So she did. She screamed so loud, it rattled the windows. But nothing happened. So she cried, forcefully enough to split her body down the middle. And she felt even less.

Diana spun the wheel, which was hot but not evil, and the dull blotches of color in that Vali of the Glens disappeared, or they became what they were before, which

Diana knew nothing about because it really didn't matter. Nothing was everything and everything was nothing
at all. In a hot metal box that moved by a wheel.

Voices began to fill the blankness in her brain, voices
joined by faces and eyes, lots of eyes, as she sailed along
with the bright, meaningless colors of red, yellow and
green. She'd heard some of them before, these voices—
she'd seen their eyes. But she didn't know why they'd be
saying what they were or why she was being watched and
followed. Watched, followed, chased and hunted. Hunted
down at lightning speed by the hauntingly familiar and
the creepily unknown. Her foot was heavy on the pedal.
So heavy it made her fly, faster and faster away from the
song of the eyes. And the voices said: *Daddy's getting tired
from all these stories…* and… *You're gonna have a real hard time
finding a man with* that *thing on your finger. It looks like an
engagement ring!* They said: *Stick with us, Diana, and we'll
have you looking as good as your mother in no time!…Well,
Diana has* been *gaining weight pretty steadily since I've known
her…There are no flowers more magical or more powerful than
azaleas…I'd have to say that the best thing to do would be to
schedule an immediate biopsy…It's like my mother used to tell
me, if you're going to let snakes roam around in your garden, at
least be sure they're wearing their raincoats…Call me TJ instead.
The only person who ever calls me Travis is my grandmother…And then you found out it wasn't cancer… Mine…
Miss Diana Fat Butt!…And then I found out it wasn't cancer…I don't know about that, Mrs. Bartle. You've got a lot of
life in you yet…Mrs. Bartle, I got the job!…I think you ought
to go see Arlene…Bird's blood! Bird's blood! Bird's Blood!…*

Here, keep it! TJ says two dollars is all you're worth!…It's Sundae Night!…Oh, would you just shut your big, fat mouth, you little freak?…Mine…Now that they're engaged, we all really think they're through playing games…azaleas…She definitely eats…And then I found out it wasn't cancer…Bartle. Everyone just called her Mrs. Bartle…My air conditioner broke. But it's supposed to be a cool night, so I thought just having the windows open would be fine…She was such a nice lady…Oh, silly me! I forgot to mention, Diana is the whore *who slept with my fiancé…Bird's blood! Bird's blood! Bird's Blood!…Mrs. Bartle has passed away…*

At 6:18 p.m., on Friday, July 11th, Diana Nicole Christopher crashed her 1994 Chevy Nova through the front window of Davey's Café on the corner of Erin Avenue and Shamrock Street in Baltimore. She was rushed to Cedar Groves Medical Center where she was treated for minor external abrasions and a fractured rib. She now lies in stabilized condition in the hospital's Psychiatric Ward, pending a mental evaluation. No motive has been determined.

It was the whitest room she had ever seen. Floors white, walls white, even the shadows were white. And Diana sat up in bed, waiting for her visitor to walk through the white door. There were no more voices, no more faces, no more eyes, and no more whispers. It was just her and the silence and the white, together and alone in the room with no color or view.

The door opened and Mrs. Christopher appeared, her face nearly as white as the room—except for the red nose and streaks of black mascara that revealed she had been crying. She remained frozen in the doorway until Diana's attempt to smile let her know that it was okay to enter. And once she did, she approached the bed slowly, as if fast footsteps would break the fragile woman on top of it. Sitting beside her daughter and taking her hand with gentle caution, Mrs. Christopher allowed her watery eyes to search Diana's face for answers. But Diana couldn't give her any, at least not yet, for she was fighting back tears of her own.

"I was out to dinner," Mrs. Christopher confessed, barely audible. "The one time I leave my cell phone at home..." Her voice drifted away for a moment. When it returned, it was louder, but faltering. "There was a message for me when I got back." Diana knew she would never be able to remember whose tears fell first but only that it was the first time that she and her mother had ever cried together. "Oh, Diana, why?" Mrs. Christopher begged, like something out of one of her bulimia fantasies. The only difference was that in the fantasies, Diana had never felt sorry for her. "Why?" her mother continued. "Why did you...do this?!" It was tremendously difficult for her to speak, and she had to hold on to her daughter's shoulders to keep from collapsing. Suddenly, Diana felt like the stronger one. She had never seen her mother go to pieces before and she wanted to take care of her.

"Mom, I didn't..." Diana began, wiping away her own tears. "The psychiatrist said I had a dissociative response to a tragedy..." Her voice was breaking up. She wanted to be clinical about this, to comfort her mother with the detached professional synopsis of what she had done, or more precisely, of what had happened *to* her—to slap any label on it that wasn't "attempted suicide"—but she couldn't. She couldn't de-personalize the incident by simply regurgitating the medical jargon the doctor had made her swallow. Not that she didn't believe it. It was just that the word *tragedy* was such an obvious euphemism for what had actually caused her response, and each time she heard it, she was reminded all too vividly of what it really meant—that Mrs. Bartle was dead.

"It's okay, Diana," her mother said, hugging her. "You don't have to talk about it."

"But I want to," Diana protested, clutching her tightly and finally knowing what it was like to be held by her mother. "Mom, I didn't try to kill myself." Mrs. Christopher pulled away slowly, staring into Diana's eyes as if she were bracing the both of them for the truth that had to be spoken. "Like I said, it was a dissociative response, which means I separated myself *from* myself, if that makes any sense."

"Not really," her mother whispered, smiling lightly, perhaps just realizing how lucky she was that Diana was even alive.

"It was like I was outside of myself, like I wasn't in control of my actions," Diana explained. "I don't remember a lot about it, really. Just a lot of fuzziness, like my eyesight was messed up. Well that, and some crazy stuff whizzing around in my brain."

"What crazy stuff?" Mrs. Christopher looked so amazingly compassionate and concerned that Diana couldn't believe she was the same woman whose very image had so often made her cringe. For the first time in her entire life, she felt like she could tell her mother anything and that she would understand. Not that she would give the best advice and know exactly how to make her feel better, like Mrs. Bartle had done for all of those years, but that she would understand. And if it weren't for the simple fact that Diana was too exhausted to explain to her mother whom all of the voices in her head had belonged to, she would have told her.

But instead, all she said was, "Memories."

"Memories?"

"Yeah. Just memories…from my life, you know?"

"Yeah," Mrs. Christopher said, stroking Diana's hair like she understood, like maybe she had crazy memories, too.

"Anyway, I ended up getting into my car, and things started coming back to me—just rushing in, all at once. I had a panic attack while I was driving…I passed out and that's when I crashed." The words made Diana feel helpless and she burst back into tears.

"Oh, baby girl," Mrs. Christopher said soothingly, lowering Diana's head onto her shoulder. She hadn't called her daughter "baby girl" since Diana really *was* a baby girl, and if Diana had taken the time to think about it, she might not have even remembered the term. But like a newborn basking in its mother's love, it seemed as if she'd never known from being called anything else.

"Mom," Diana continued, sobbing. "Mrs. Bartle is…*dead!*" The last word emerged hysterically as Diana tightened her shaking hands into little fists and covered her face, like the glass was going to shatter around her again. She couldn't stand to use that ugly word—a word so unmerciful, so final, cold and cruel—in relation to Mrs. Bartle.

"Mrs. Bartle? That sweet old lady from upstairs?" Mrs. Christopher asked.

"It was DOWNSTAIRS!" Diana screamed, lifting her face to meet her mother's, suddenly infuriated for all the times she'd made that mistake or, worse yet, forgotten Mrs. Bartle's name entirely. "She was my *best friend!*"

"Diana, I'm sorry—"

"No, *I'm* sorry!" Her voice had risen to a shrill screech. "I'm sorry that my best friend is dead! I'm sorry that Daddy's dead! I'm sorry that I killed him! I'm sorry that—"The pain in her mother's eyes caused her to stop screaming. It was a familiar kind of pain, like the kind Diana could feel reflecting through her own eyes when-ever she thought about her father, the kind that was probably there right now, mirroring her mother's. "I'm sorry that I embarrassed you," Diana continued softly, lowering her eyes to the bed, "when I cried for Bernie that one time."

"Bernie?"

"Yeah, remember Bernie with the drinking problem? How he died in the street and no one cared and I ran out there screaming in front of all the neighbors?"

"Diana," Mrs. Christopher said, smiling gently, as she smoothed some hair away from her daughter's face, "Bernie was an ex-con who had served three years in prison for beating his pregnant girlfriend so badly she miscarried. His poor, sick mother had taken him in when he was paroled because he couldn't afford a place of his own, and he thanked her by blowing her social security checks on bar tabs. Did you know that the neighbors used to take turns driving her to pick up her prescriptions because Bernie was always too hung over to do it himself?"

Diana shook her head. If she had known any of this, she never would have bothered waving to him on her walks home from school or getting out of bed every night to watch him stumble away from the cab.

"Of course you didn't know. You were just a little girl then, and you wouldn't have understood… The little girl with the strawberry curls," Mrs. Christopher said, twirling Diana's hair around on her finger with a sentimental smile. "I should've told you about Bernie when you got older. But I never knew you still carried it around. You never mentioned it, so I must have figured you'd forgotten. I had."

"There were a lot of things I never mentioned, Mom." Diana spoke softly. She wanted to be careful with the truth, to use it not as a weapon to create new wounds, but as a way to possibly heal some old ones. More than anything, she just wanted to keep talking honestly like this—with her mom. It was something they'd never really tried before.

"I know," Mrs. Christopher sighed, looking down as she took Diana's hand. "And that's my fault, too." She took a breath as if she were about to say something else, but then she paused, looking up, suddenly confused. "Diana, why did you say you killed your daddy? Your father died in a car accident. You know that."

"I know," Diana said. "But he died because…" She'd never said it out loud before, and her heart was pounding the same way it had when she was six and she thought her mother already knew. And although she'd never gotten over believing that, her fear of getting in trouble for it had decreased over the years. But now that she was about to admit it, she was frightened of the consequences. For her mother's wrathful reaction could only be worse now than it would have been when her daughter was six and she was still legally obligated to care for her. Perhaps more frightening than anything, however, was that slight chance that maybe her mother didn't know anything about it at all. Taking a deep breath, Diana forced herself to finish the confession. "Because I kept making him read me more stories even though I knew he was tired and had a really long drive ahead of him."

"Oh, Diana, honey, I knew that!" Mrs. Christopher exclaimed, waving her off without the slightest evidence of shock.

"You did?"

"Of course! You did stuff like that all the time."

"I did?"

"Sure," her mother said, shaking her head as if completely confounded by her daughter's failure to remember what appeared to have been a constant childhood habit. "You were wonderful at manipulating us. We'd come to expect it. Of course, I do remember one time when you really pulled a fast one on me."

"A fast one?"

"Oh, you were *gooood*," her mother joked, peering at Diana slyly from the corner of her eye. "You even got to me most of the time, and I was supposed to be the disciplinarian!" She laughed. "Your father, now, he was the old softie. He *never* said no to you." It felt strange to hear her mother admit to being the stricter parent, for although she obviously was, Diana had never imagined that she'd been that way because somebody needed to be. She'd always just assumed that Daddy was warm because he loved her a lot and that Mommy was cold because she loved her a lot less. "Anyway, this one time," Mrs. Christopher continued, "you made me so late for dinner at my aunt Laura's that she fell asleep waiting for me with her face flat on the dining room table and a piece of fettuccine stretching from her mouth all the way to the floor!" Her mother giggled at the image. "Oh, Diana, she was so mad at me—until I told her why I was late, and then she forgave me. 'Patty,' she said, 'don't you ever deny that little girl the joy of being read to by her mother. I don't care if you're two *days* late next time instead of just two hours. That little girl of yours is worth it.'"

"Didn't Aunt Laura die?"

"Yes, Diana, but not because you were a little girl who liked bedtime stories," Mrs. Christopher reassured her, taking Diana's face in her hands like she was once again a little girl who needed Mommy to tell her that things would be okay. "And that's not why your daddy died either."

"But if I hadn't—"

"Diana, there's something I never told you about your father's death," her mother interrupted. Diana's eyes grew wide with curiosity, the kind that makes one both crave and dread the truth. "Your father..." Mrs. Christopher took a deep breath. "About three months before he died, your daddy got sick. So we took him to a doctor—a psychiatrist—and, uh…" Diana watched as her mother struggled to compose herself. She was trembling, and for the first time ever, Diana felt closer to her than she did to the father she missed every day of her life. Perhaps it was because she and her mother were still here, discovering that they had more in common—more pain, more memories, more love and more fear—than either of them had ever taken the time to realize.

"Mom, it's okay."

"I know, honey," her mother said, grabbing her daughter's hand tightly and with a courageous smile, as if Diana's hand were all she needed to go on. "Diana, your father suffered from severe anxiety. And I don't mean the kind that makes you have trouble sleeping and gives you that feeling of panic in social situations—although he suffered from both of those things. But it was far worse than that."

"Well, how bad was it?"

"He would, um…sometimes, he would start to hallucinate." The tears began to spill again from Mrs. Christopher's eyes. "He'd see things that weren't there and flip out about stuff that had never really happened."

Diana shook her head from side to side, fighting a memory she'd always dismissed as a bad dream. "That time…" she began, "that time when I came home from kindergarten and all the lights were out and the curtains completely drawn…and we found Daddy in the basement…hiding in the storage closet…" Mrs. Christopher nodded slowly, closing her eyes over her tears. "He was whispering," Diana continued. "Something about…some people…the…" Diana struggled to remember the name.

"The Linderbachs are coming," her mother said softly, looking over Diana's shoulder, as if into another time.

"Who were the Linderbachs?"

"I never found out… Most likely nobody, just people that his mind made up for him to be scared of." Her mother looked back into her eyes apologetically. "I told you it was a bad dream. I just didn't want you to look at your daddy the way I was starting to."

"Mom, it's all right," Diana consoled her. "I forgive you."

"You do?" Mrs. Christopher looked stunned.

"Of course, I do. I'm glad I didn't know. I mean, you could have told me before now, but I'm glad I didn't know then."

"He wanted help, Diana, he really did," her mother continued, straightening herself up and wiping her eyes. "He didn't want to lose his family—that was the one fear that didn't come from his head. It came from his heart. You—and me, too, but especially you—you meant everything to him. Anyway, um—" her voice began to waver "—the night your father left you at Mrs. Kingsly's to come spend the weekend down the shore with me for our anniversary…well…I never knew anything about that…I was driving home from work when I saw the flames." Mrs. Christopher covered her mouth and tried desperately to catch her breath. It was like she could see the fire in front of her again, like she was seeing it for the first time. "There were sirens all over the place—police, ambulance, fire trucks. And although I couldn't even make out what kind of car it was, I just got this terrible feeling. There was a cop conducting traffic, but he wouldn't answer anyone's questions. I watched him shrug his shoulders at the driver in front of me, and all he said was, 'They haven't identified the body yet.'"

"Oh, God!" Diana cried out, raising her hands to her own mouth in horror. Although she had envisioned it so many times, the image she'd created of her father's accident now seemed like a cartoon compared to these brutal details she'd never heard before—like all of those terrifying sirens and her father being the unidentified "body" engulfed in a traffic-blocking sea of flames.

"I came home to a note," her mother continued softly, looking down at the bed. "It said that you were around the corner at Mrs. Kingsly's and that he'd told you he was leaving to meet me for an anniversary weekend down the shore, that he'd tried calling me at work but must have just missed me, and that I should go to the second floor, west wing waiting room of St. Peter's Hospital so that we could discuss some possible excuses for where he'd be for the next few weeks, or months, or however long it was going to take." Mrs. Christopher looked up and into her daughter's eyes. "He ended by saying 'I love you' and 'Please don't tell Diana where I am, just that Daddy loves her very much and will miss her every day that he's gone.'"

"So the day he left me with Mrs. Kingsly…" Diana began slowly, trying to piece together twenty-six years of darkness with the single light of truth she'd just been given.

"He was going to check himself in for treatment," her mother finished for her. "I got the call that he was dead about fifteen minutes after I read the note."

"Well, what did you do in those fifteen minutes before you knew?" Diana asked.

"I cried," her mother said, "because I already knew. You had to drive over those train tracks in order to get to St. Peter's. I just knew after I read the note that the car was his. And I didn't want to leave the house because I didn't want to miss the call."

"Mom, I'm so sorry. If I had known…" Diana didn't know what to say. She didn't know what she would have done had she known the whole truth before now.

Mrs. Christopher smiled sadly. "If you had known, then I wouldn't have honored what I believed to have been your father's last wish."

"Then thanks for not telling me," Diana said. And she meant it. But after a few moments of silence, a terrible thought crossed her mind. "So, do you think that Daddy meant to—"

"Sometimes," her mother interrupted, saving Diana from having to finish the awful sentence herself. "But other times I think that maybe he had another hallucination and lost control of the car. The truth is that I don't know." Mrs. Christopher looked exhausted and, for the first time ever, she looked old, or at least as old as any woman who'd carried around such a heartwrenching secret for over a quarter of a century would look. "The newspapers said it was an accident, that it seemed he had fallen asleep driving," she continued. "And since your father had never been formally diagnosed with anything more than an anxiety problem, I never told anyone about the hallucinations he was on his way to get help for. And I never showed anyone the note. Diana, there's probably a very good chance that your father was schizophrenic. But if *we* never knew that for sure, why should other people have had the chance to speculate about it after he was gone? He was a wonderful man, Diana. He really was. And sick or not at the very end, his memory deserved the same dignity as any other good man."

"Well, you gave that to him," Diana said, looking her mother straight in the eye to let her know how much she meant it.

"Thank you," Mrs. Christopher whispered, holding her hand to her heart. "You know, you remind me a lot of him—the good parts, I mean, before he got sick."

"I do?"

"Oh, so much." Her mother smiled. "The way you tell a story, the way you laugh, the way you show it, but think you hide it, when you want the whole world to go to hell." Diana laughed. "Your wit," her mother continued, "your loyalty, your ability to find that one true friend and really treasure her, like you did with Mrs. Bartle. But what's really worried me over the years has been your dark side, your brooding side, the one that makes you withdraw from the world. Your father had that, too. And on one hand, it was wonderful. It meant that he was sensitive and thoughtful and deeply unique—all of the things that you are, all of the things that made me love both of you. But that dark side can betray you. It can make you hurt yourself. And I guess that's why, since I missed the chance to save your daddy from his, I was always trying so hard to save you from yours. Although, I'm sure I went about it the wrong way," Mrs. Christopher said, laughing lightly.

"You drove me nuts," Diana admitted.

"And when you're a mother, you'll do that to your kids. I just wanted you to be happy. So I started with the outside, with the most obvious problem that I thought I could help you fix, which was your—"

"Weight," Diana interjected, at the exact moment that her mother was concluding with the very same sentiment. They smiled at each other—a warm, genuine, and incredibly refreshing smile that Diana never imagined they would share over the subject of her weight. "I'm sorry I pushed you away."

"It's okay. I'd have pushed me away, too," her mother said with a laugh.

"I guess after Daddy died, I never really wanted to get too close. I think I was worried I might lose you, too."

"It's okay, honey," Mrs. Christopher said, reaching out gently to tuck a strand of hair behind Diana's ear. "I think that in my own way, I did the same thing."

"I love you, Mom," Diana said. She knew the words should have felt strange, but for some reason they didn't— they were the only words that seemed right.

"Oh, I love you too, baby," her mother said, pulling her close for a hug and exhaling a deep sigh of relief. "I'm just so glad you're okay…with everything."

"I am," Diana said softly, resting her head on her

mother's shoulder and feeling more relaxed than she had in a long time.

"Good. Because there's something else I haven't told you yet."

"What?" Diana asked, lifting herself up suddenly. "What is it?"

"You're getting *skinny,*" Mrs. Christopher said, poking her daughter's shoulder playfully.

Diana had waited most of her life to hear these words, but somehow, although they were a pleasant runner-up, they still didn't mean as much as *I love you.* She leaned back against her pillow. Her eyelids felt heavy, but she had one more question to ask, one more answer she needed to find before she could rest.

"Mom?" she asked, struggling to keep her eyes open. "Who's going to take care of me now that Mrs. Bartle is gone?"

Mrs. Christopher stroked her daughter's hair as she watched her fall fast asleep without even waiting for an answer. Perhaps she already knew it. But just in case there was some tiny part of consciousness still listening, a part that might filter through to Diana's dreams and make them sweeter, Mrs. Christopher, in the process of leaning over to kiss her daughter's forehead, first stopped to whisper in her ear the words, "*I* will." And being able to say them was *her* pleasant runner-up to *I love you.*

The warm, shadowy streaks that stretched across Diana's eyelids made her curious enough to open them.

It was the sun. They'd moved her to another room, one that had a window.

"I guess I'm no longer crazy," she mumbled to herself, her throat dry from sleep.

"Well, that depends on who you ask," said a voice to her right. Diana turned around. It was Barry, sitting by her bed.

"Hi," she said shyly, wondering if it would be okay to show that never in her life had she been this grateful to see anyone else. There was just something in his voice, something in those deep brown eyes and that incredibly warm smile that said he understood her and liked her anyway.

"Hi… Rough night?"

Diana smiled. "How did you know I was here?"

"Well, after I got the news about, you know, Aunt Rose…" Barry cleared his throat, swallowing hard. "I, uh…well, I tried to find you at your place, but you weren't there. So, I looked your mother up in the phone book. She wasn't home, but I got her cell phone number from the answering machine, and when I called her, she was here."

Diana couldn't believe he'd gone to all the trouble. If only the news that had driven him to it hadn't been so awful, then maybe she'd be able to consider the possibilities of what his going to all that trouble actually meant. But it *was* awful news that had brought them together.

"Barry, I'm so sorry about Mrs….your aunt."

"You know, she always thought it was cute that you called her Mrs. Bartle."

"She did?"

"Yeah. But she liked it. I think it made her feel like Mrs. Garrett in 'The Facts of Life,' or maybe Mr. Miyagi in *The Karate Kid*—like she was wise and somebody's mentor. I mean, she would've been fine with you just calling her Rose, but there was still that small part of her that was probably glad you didn't. Maybe because Bartle was the name my great-uncle, Henry, gave to her. She probably liked hearing it repeated…" Barry paused. It was as if he wished he had more to say, like maybe if he kept talking, neither of them would have to acknowledge the wealth of emptiness that was about to become a permanent part of their lives now that Mrs. Bartle no longer was. But he didn't have more to say. All he could do was look away from her in silence, his eyes shining with unshed tears.

"Oh, Barry. I'm sorry," Diana said. "I really am sorry."

"Why didn't she tell me?" he asked. His tone was both desperate and pleading—as if the answer to his question could change fate—but still, he looked away, toward some place across the room where miracles might grow.

"Tell you what?" Diana asked gently.

Barry turned suddenly to face her. His stare was incredulous and haunted by heartache. "About the air conditioner," he said, his voice breaking. "I could have flown back early. It's only fucking business! She…she…" He ran his hands through his hair in anguished frustration, catching his breath.

"Barry, she knew that," Diana said, hoping her words would comfort him. "She told me you were coming in at the end of the week and would fix it for her. I wanted to go buy her one, even, but she said no. She said she only—"

"I know," he said, relaxing a little. "She only put the air on for company." They smiled at each other sadly, remembering her quirky charm. "She still should have told me. I spoke to her twice this week and she never even mentioned it."

"She probably just didn't want to worry you. Barry, she probably didn't even think it was anything *worth* worrying over. I don't think Mrs. Bartle would have purposely risked not being around for us."

Relief washed briefly over Barry's face, as if he'd just been pardoned from a guilt he'd have never known how to break free from on his own. He'd found truth in Diana's consolation, and for a moment it was enough to comfort him. But then he seemed to remember his grief, and his demeanor changed again—to one of great sorrow. He looked at Diana as if there was still something missing—a question that had to be asked.

"What is it?" she wanted to know.

"She was my best friend," Barry said. And to him, it was a question. He'd wanted to ask how life could go on without her, but hadn't been able to form the words. This was as close as he could get, but Diana understood the language of loss and knew exactly what he meant, though she couldn't answer him—his questions were the same as hers.

"I know," she said softly. "Mine, too."

Barry laid his head down on her hand, allowing his tears to fall through her fingers onto the blanket. With her free hand, Diana smoothed his hair and felt what it was like to take care of somebody else. Suddenly she had the impulse to scoop up all of his pain and make it her own. She knew, of course, that this wasn't possible. But if it were, she would do it, which was a totally unfamiliar inclination considering that she usually believed she possessed enough pain to distribute evenly amongst all non-suffering citizens of the western world, with still enough left over to keep herself more than humble. Still, here she was, wishing she could completely take away someone else's and yet knowing all the while that she was still irreversibly bound to her own.

It was a couple of minutes before Barry lifted his head and leaned back in his chair again. And then he scratched his face—not to satisfy an itch it seemed, but perhaps to create a transition gesture from which he could slip from the role of Man in Grief back into Witty, Wonderful, and Sincere Old Barry without actually having to acknowledge the breakdown. Diana understood. It was hard for men to cry. However, the fact that he had could never be forgotten, for it had brought to her attention a possibility she'd never allowed herself to recognize, not when she was seventeen, and certainly not when he resurfaced in Mrs. Bartle's living room: she might love him.

"So," Barry began, glancing over at her briefly and continuing to scratch his face, "I hear you gave the Baltimore police quite a run for their money last night."

"What do you mean?"

"I *mean*…" Barry had started to smile a little. "You're

the only woman I've ever known—no, make that the only *person* I've ever known—that's been involved in a high-speed car chase with the police. Unless, of course, that was your stunt double in the car."

"What on earth are you talking about?"

"You really don't know?" Barry looked surprised. "Diana, the police were following you. One of the paramedics at Glen Vali put a call into the station when he saw you speed away. You had two squad cars trying to block you in when you gunned it past both of them and crashed into that café." Now that he mentioned it, she did remember hearing sirens. "We're lucky you weren't seriously hurt."

His words sent a panic through Diana, forcing her to worry about something that, astonishingly enough, hadn't occurred to her before now. "Was anyone else hurt? On the road? Or in the café?"

"Just you, my dear, with your scrapes and sore ribs," he said, running his finger lightly across the bandage on her right arm. "There was one minor fender bender reported—one car rear-ending another when their light turned green and you sped across the intersection on red, but all that came out of that was a loose license plate. Both drivers were fine."

"But what about Davey's? Was anyone in there when I—?"

"No." Barry rescued her. "I mean, yes, but…have you ever been inside the café?" Diana looked at him strangely. Barry smiled, embarrassed. "Sorry, bad choice of words. I mean, have you ever patronized the establishment…

gone in for coffee or something?" Diana shook her head. "Okay, well your car entered through the front window," Barry explained. "That's where the cash register is, the coffee machines, the dessert case, maybe a tacky fake plant or two. But the tables are set up in a separate room entirely."

"And so there wasn't anybody up front when it happened?"

"No, not up front," Barry said, "but there was one boy—"

"Boy?" Diana was frightened. What boy? She thought Barry had said no one was hurt.

"Well, not exactly a boy," Barry said, squinting towards the ceiling as if deep in speculation, "but not really a man either...although I'm sure he'd beg to differ," he finished, looking Diana straight in the eye. She could see that he was joking.

"Barry," she pleaded.

"He was probably sixteen."

"Barry..."

"Or maybe seventeen. But, like, a *young* seventeen."

"Barry?"

"Yeah?" he asked, breaking away from his banter to assume a look of naiveté, like he hadn't a single clue as to why she'd be rushing him through his detailed physical description of the boy-man at the café.

"What *about* him?"

"Oh!... Well...he's fine." Diana raised her eyebrows, signaling that she was still waiting for a better answer. Barry smiled, giving in. "He was working alone and was supposed to be manning the register, but since he only had a few customers and they'd just been served, he figured there was time to go out and catch a smoke. He saw the whole thing happen through the back door."

"Oh, my God," Diana said, looking down as the chills raced through her. She couldn't believe she'd come that close to hurting someone. She couldn't believe how lucky she was that she hadn't. She looked back up at Barry, confused. "How do you know all of this?"

"I saw it on the news," he said matter-of-factly. "*And* I've been sitting in the waiting room with your mother since one o'clock this morning… She told me what the doctors said."

"Oh, my God!" Diana gasped, burying her face in her hands in a combined display of shock and embarrassment. "I don't know what's worse—the fact that I was on the news for all of Baltimore to know I'm a basket case or the fact that the man I'm interested in just spent God only knows how many hours talking to my *mother.*" The words escaped her mouth before she had a chance to analyze them, and now that she'd spoken, she really wished she hadn't said anything at all. *The man I'm interested in*—the phrase echoed in her mind, over and over, filling her face with color. And she waited, for what seemed like another God-only-knows-how-many-hours, for Barry—the man she was *interested* in—to tease her or, worse yet, do nothing at all. But he only smiled—in a way that seemed to be neither of the two and, at the very same time, an even mixture of each. And then they locked eyes, and Barry ran his thumb over the knuckles on Diana's right hand. And despite the fact that she was wearing a faded hospital gown accented only by bruises and bandages, and that she and Barry were holding hands in the least romantic setting she could have ever imagined for such a magical moment to take place, his touch sent shivers to parts of her body that seemed to have been asleep since before she was born. And he didn't need to say anything at all—because this moment said everything. There was nothing to be embarrassed about.

Diana spoke first. "Does my mother know that you're the same Barry that took my virginity at the Suttons' New Year's Eve party?"

"Is *that* why she asked for my phone number?" Barry joked. Diana laughed, wondering how it was possible that someone so funny, successful and sincere could also be so handsome—and so interested in her. "Actually, I think she does know," he continued seriously. "But I don't think it bothers her."

"How come?"

"Because you're not seventeen anymore, and this isn't 1988…and I don't think it hurts that she knows how much I care about you."

"And how does she know that?" Diana asked, her heart tingling from his words.

"I told you, I was in the waiting room with her since one o'clock in the morning. Do you think we only talked about the accident?" Diana didn't know what to think. And for perhaps the first time in her life, she thought maybe it was okay to just *be*—without all the self-analysis and dissection of everyone else's actions. Maybe for once she wouldn't have to translate what another person's words were secretly or subconsciously saying about her. Maybe for once she trusted that she was worthy of being cared for without wondering about hidden motives or candid cameras. She was finally accepting herself without any strings. And she felt free. "By the way," Barry said, "Davey's won't be pressing any charges."

"Did my mother tell you that?"

"No, my lawyer did. I called him and asked if he'd represent you in the event that they did want to make a case out of it," Barry explained. "But as it turns out, we won't be needing his services. Mr. 'Davey' will make enough money from the insurance settlement and, apparently, whoever he is, he has a conscience and doesn't feel the need to go after your pockets—that is, the pockets of a woman with a medical excuse for what happened, a medical excuse that my attorney reminded *his* attorney came straight from the diagnosis of one of this city's leading psychiatrists, and not only that, but also from within the well-respected walls of one of this fair state's top five hospitals."

"Barry," Diana whispered, shaking her head in amazement over the great lengths he'd traveled amidst a family tragedy just to spare her further pain.

"I hope you don't mind I let the word out that those pockets probably weren't very deep, anyway," Barry said, wincing playfully as if she might punch him for it.

But Diana was far from angry. "How can I thank you?" she asked.

"Come to work for me," Barry said quickly, as if he'd

been holding in the request for months, just waiting for her to ask a question like that.

"What?"

"How are you with typing and filing and answering phones?"

"No experience whatsoever," Diana said, wondering how in the world Barry had come up with this idea and where the catch was.

"Perfect." He smiled. "I was actually about to place an ad in the paper for someone with no experience whatsoever. You've saved me a lot of trouble."

"Barry, what is this about?"

"Honestly?" he asked, becoming serious. Diana nodded. "My aunt, Rose."

"I don't understand," Diana said softly. It hurt to hear Mrs. Bartle's name. But Barry's being there made it a lot easier.

"She made me promise to ask you to work for me when my Baltimore shop opens. Kind of as my secretary-slash–office manager-slash...whatever," Barry said, shrugging his shoulders. Diana was speechless. Even though her best friend was no longer there, it was as if she was—still looking out for her like she always had. "Now, she also made me promise not to pressure you," Barry continued, "because you just got this great new job working with kids, which is something you're really excited about." Diana didn't know why, but at this least appropriate moment in time, she was suddenly overcome by an all-consuming urge to burst out laughing. Maybe it was because in light of all the truly tragic things that had transpired

272   *Lindsay Faith Rech*

or revealed themselves in the last twenty-four hours, her
spazzing out on the penis-butt child suddenly seemed like
comic relief, a memory that, if recalled in the proper style,
could even make a funny story someday. "Anyway," Barry
kept going, "she thought that if the nursery school thing
didn't work out for the fall, you might like to come work
for me when camp was over." Diana couldn't contain herself any longer. Gasping to catch her breath, she finally
broke free, exploding with laughter—and it felt terrific.
"So, here I am…" Barry said slowly, staring at her with
a bulgy-eyed kind of pretend paranoia that only made
Diana laugh harder "…asking, but not pressuring," he
continued, feigning caution, as if Diana were something
to both study and fear.

"Oh, Barry, I got fired!" she managed to yell out, as she
wiped the tears of laughter from the corners of her eyes.

"Great!" he exclaimed, exaggeratedly happy, throwing
his hands in the air to match her mood.

"You don't understand," Diana said breathlessly, waving him off, too exhausted to explain. Barry caught her
hand before it retreated, kissing it gently and once again
sending shivers to previously unalive areas of her anatomy,
areas that hadn't even been kindled the first time they
touched hands a couple minutes earlier. It made her wonder what parts of her body would wake up next.

"You're hired," he said, rising. "Mind if I open the curtains a little wider to get some more light in here?"

"Go ahead," Diana said, turning her head as her eyes
followed him to the window. "You know, you could just
turn on the light—" Her words got caught in her throat

when she beheld the crystal vase on the windowsill. It was full of azaleas.

"I got them this morning," Barry said shyly. "Do you like them?"

"I had a dream," Diana whispered, staring fixedly at the flowers with a faraway look in her eyes, entranced. "It must have been just after I crashed… My father—" She paused suddenly, remembering what she'd learned from her mother. This was the first time she would ever look at the Daddy that lived in her dreams—superhero, angel, answer-to-her-prayers Daddy—not through the starry eyes of a six-year-old girl but through the unshielded eyes of a grown woman who knew the truth. The realization drew the corners of her mouth up into a bittersweet smile. She smiled sadly because she now knew how much he had suffered, but with extra love for the flaws that had made him human. "My father…he was standing there in a circle of light, beautiful light, pointing at something I couldn't see and waving me backward… It was kind of like the dream I had with the garden, except that time I could see what he was pointing to—I knew what he wanted. This time I was so confused. I wondered if he still loved me… Last time, he was welcoming me in with open arms, and now he was telling me I shouldn't have come. But then I saw his lips moving and I knew he was trying to tell me something. So I stopped wondering what was happening, and I strained to listen… And what he said made me realize I wasn't supposed to die yet."

"What did he say?"

"He said, 'Azaleas grow in heaven, too,'" Diana whispered, still captivated by the flowers on the sill. "He didn't need me to bring him any this time."

Barry watched her for a while in silence until a question occurred to him. "What do you think he was pointing to when he was waving you back?"

"Honestly?" Diana asked, turning her attention away from the window. Barry nodded. "You." The idea hadn't occurred to her until now, but it made logical sense—her father was pointing to a reason for her to stick around. And it was a wonderful reason.

"Are you sure it was a dream?"

"No," Diana answered truthfully. And the two of them remained still and quiet, allowing the magnitude of all that had happened—in their lives and in this very moment— to touch them and fly away...because this was about new beginnings.

It was a little while before Barry moved to return to his seat. And as he lowered his body to the chair, he paused suddenly to throw his arms around Diana. They held each other tightly, so tightly that breathing was almost out of the question, but neither of them seemed any the worse for it. When Barry did sit back down, he reached underneath his chair and retrieved a small blanket.

"She was holding this when they found her," he said, handing it to Diana. It was the baby blanket she'd started making the night Mrs. Bartle had tried to teach her how to knit—the one her friend had said would be her greatest pleasure to finish so that she could give it to Diana as a present. Diana's hands trembled as she laid the blanket across her lap to look at it, and her eyes filled with tears

at what she saw. It was a memento of their last week together, the one they'd spent working to keep Diana's
mind off TJ—the last week they would ever share:

In one corner was a picture of two playing cards from
the first night when they'd rediscovered the fun of simple games like War and Go Fish. In another corner was
the prince from *Cinderella,* and at the bottom was an ice-
cream sundae. And knitted in beautiful pink script across
the center were the words: *Through Princes and War and
Sundae Night Thursdays, I love you!—Mrs. B.*

Diana held the blanket to her chest and closed her eyes,
allowing the week Mrs. Bartle had so eloquently captured
in yarn to unravel itself like a montage in her mind.

"There's something on the other side," Barry said once
she opened her eyes again.

Diana turned the blanket over to see that knitted on
the back were a pair of silvery-blue, high-heeled shoes
and the inscription: *P.S.—You can't run away in glass slippers!* Remembering what she'd told Mrs. Bartle after
they'd watched *Cinderella*—that if she had a pair of glass
slippers and a prince to put them on her feet, she'd never
want to run away from herself again—she handed the
blanket back to Barry.

"Will you lay this across my feet and not ask why?"

Barry smiled adoringly, like maybe he already knew
why, like maybe he even thought it was a little silly, but
he honored Diana's wish without a single word, proving
with his silence how much he really cared.

"Thank you," she whispered, smiling gratefully.

Barry took her hand. "You know, I should probably go

get your mom and tell her you're awake," he said. "She's gonna want to see you."

"Just stay with me for a few more minutes," Diana pleaded gently, squeezing his hand as she turned to face the azaleas on the windowsill. And as the two of them sat there, gazing at the brilliant sea of color that streamed through the crystal vase and hugged the pink flowers with light, Diana realized that, with a little help from Mrs. Bartle, she had just found her prince.

August 16th

"Today is the first day of the rest of your life."

Dear Diary,

I used to think that saying was a stupid cliché, but I believe it with all my heart now. My life has been full of second chances—the tumor that turned out to be benign, the car crash that didn't kill me…even Barry. Fifteen years ago, I dismissed him as a one-night stand, somebody I'd never see again. But yet, I never stopped thinking about him. Sex in the freezing cold in the back of a pickup truck… Most women would choose to forget that memory in exchange for a "first time" with rose petals and commitment. Instead, I carried it around—like a proud, dirty badge under my clothes. Maybe it was because that's all I ever had, but seeing how things have turned out, I think it was more than that. Of course, I'm not even sure that Fate would have approved enough of the way we met to orchestrate our bizarre reunion. After all, one brief night of automotive passion between a minor and a man nearly thirty is hardly the basis for a fairy tale. But I certainly have some force to thank. Being with Barry makes me happier than I've ever been before, and the second chance has been long worth the wait.

It's now been five weeks since Mrs. Bartle passed away. I keep her blanket draped over the foot of my bed during the day, and at night I fall asleep holding it. "Through Princes and War and Sundae Night Thursdays…"—the words sometimes enter my dreams. But they are with me most especially when I am awake, reminding me of how well she knew me and of how far I've come. I did have my share of princes—my father, who was going to whisk me away to a happier place on a tumor blimp; TJ, who was going to make me a sexy siren that men just couldn't resist; and now, the one she sent to me bearing glass slippers, her great-nephew Barry, the one least likely and the one that was meant to be. The peace he has brought me has made me realize how senseless the wars were. My biggest war was always with myself, namely my weight. But when I see myself through Barry's eyes—those deep brown, loving eyes that see me as beautiful—I know that hating my body is a silly waste of time and that it would hurt him to hear me bashing it, just as it would hurt me to know that he hated any part of himself. [PS I've lost eight more pounds, which brings me to 148 (which is a total of thirty pounds, and only eighteen pounds away

from that goal weight I used to mention—not to be con-
fused with my being just one *jean size away from the tens*
I promised myself I'd buy with my refund on that ring I
returned to EasyShop…but who's even counting any-
more?)]. And I'm proud to say that I've heeded Mrs. Bar-
tle's good advice and have yet to spend a single Thursday
night Sundaeless since the tradition began. Perhaps that's
the secret of my success.

I'm even out of the warring zone with my mother,
who I must say earned major brownie points when Barry
told me he saw her snagging this journal away from the
Cedar Groves medical staff. A while after the police re-
trieved my personal belongings from the glove compartment,
some "well-intended" professionals "stumbled" upon them
at the nurses' station. My mother had just emerged from
the ladies' room when she found the doctors paging through
this, "unsure" of what it was and of what further clues it
might give them as to the state of my psyche. Apparently,
she totally let 'em have it! Barry had just gotten there and
didn't even know that the woman making a fuss was my
mother. It's comforting to know that she stood up for my
right to privacy, not that I can guarantee that she *didn't*
read it afterward, but she hasn't been looking at me
strangely, so I'm pretty confident that she didn't. We've ac-
tually been spending a lot of time together lately. She even
joined me for a class at Mo's Gym, but I think I was right
about that—line dancing to the Bee Gees just isn't her
speed. But she's being supportive of my decision not to
reenter hyperactive-waifs-in-spandex land, and I'm being
supportive of her decision not to force herself into doing any-

thing that makes her feel like a bumbling fool that can't keep up. Actually, my mother and I are just very support-ive of one another in general now. We're working toward a "symbiotic" relationship, one in which our individual dif-ferences are mutually beneficial to both parties—and we're doing it in therapy once a week through a psychologist the hospital recommended, one that I also see once a week on my own. And we always go out for lunch afterward to re-ward our successful sessions. Overall, I'd say I'm learning to let her be a mother, no longer resisting "for the sake of mere resistance," as Dr. Dewison so aptly put it, and I'm even making a new friend in the process. She can still bug the hell out of me with just one look, but it's happening less and less, and I guess that if it didn't happen at all, she wouldn't be Mom.

Of course, no one will ever be able to replace Mrs. Bartle. I miss her every day. Sometimes I burst into tears for no reason, like when I'm watching a stupid talk show or folding the laundry. But then I remember that there is a reason—that Mrs. Bartle is gone—and I cry even harder. I know that what gets me through it is Barry and the safe and heart-happy feeling I get whenever he's around, which is most of the time. And my mother helps, too. She's been very "supportive" since the beginning… The beginning— it's strange how I've reversed my thinking. Everything al-ways used to seem like a whirlwind, spiraling—with me in it—towards some kind of very dark place, some dreaded end. And now it's just the opposite. It's as if Mrs. Bartle gave me a brand-new world when she left, and brand-new eyes to see it with. Or maybe it's me. I haven't told anyone this—not even Barry, who loves me no matter what, or Dr. Dewison, who gets paid to—but I don't truly believe that Mrs. Bartle is gone. I know she still watches out for me, sitting up there with Henry and my father on some white, fluffy cloud, waiting for me to get married and have babies and live a wonderful life.

As for Barry and I, it's funny. We haven't even had sex yet (at least not in this millennium). We're taking the physical stuff slowly, which is nice for two reasons. One, because we're really falling in love, which will make it all the more special when we do take that step. And two, I'll have gotten so much thinner by the time he actually does see me naked than I was when we first started dating. But then again, "dating" isn't really the right term for two people that have already discussed marriage. But since we are taking it slow, I guess dating is what we'll call it for now.

And since this diary is just about filled, I'll have to start a new one when Barry and I begin our new chapter. But for now, I'm happy to leave off in the chapter that we're on—because it gives this book that I started after my first second chance a pretty happy ending. It might not be a fairy tale's "And they lived happily ever after," but it's one of reality's nearest equivalents and the absolute closest I've ever gotten. I guess the best part of all is that, unlike Cinderella, Sleeping Beauty, Snow White, and anyone else that has ever lived "happily ever after," none of my story is make-believe…and it's incredibly far from over!

Diana